The Ocotillo Review

Volume 6.2

The Ocotillo Review Volume 6.2
©2022 Kallisto Gaaia Press Inc.
All Rights Reserved

Attention Schools and businesses: For discounted prices on large orders please contact the publisher directly.
Kallisto Gaia Press Inc.
1801 E. 51st Street
Suite 365-246
Austin TX 78723
info@kallistogaiapress.org
(254) 654-7205

Cover Photo: Mary Day Long

Edited by Tony Burnett

ISSN: 2573-4113
ISBN: 978-1-952224-23-2

The

Ocofillo

Review

Volume 6.2
"Mistakes"

Summer 2022

FICTION · POETRY · TRUTH

Editorial Board

The Ocotillo Review is supported in part by a grant from the City of Austin Cultural Arts Department

TABLE OF CONTENTS

Poetry

Fiction

Truth

Precious Reader,

Here we are. This marks the eleventh edition of your favorite literary journal, *The Ocotillo Review*. I can't thank you enough for the years of support we continue to garner from the ever-expanding literary community.

We have new work from some of our favorite poets and writers who've graced our pages in past issues including **Gordon Brown**'s hilarious "ghost" story, **Marc Hess** with an international thriller, **Federica Santini** with a pair of brief but powerful feminist tomes, new surrealist poetry from **John Bradley**, **Dan Smart** with another poem from his upcoming collection, and **Milton Jordan**'s thoughts on our basic toolbox. We are also privileged to showcase some phenomenal voices for the first time in our pages. **Austin Smith** has a new take on our lunar fixation, **Montana Agte-Studier** warns us of Gaia's ability to take charge if we fail to honor her power, **Oscar Rodriguez** takes us on a wild ride through Colorado, **Charmaine Arjoonlal** shares the joys and hardships of life way off the grid in the Yukon, **Richard Holinger** dreams of old girlfriends and **Laurie Blauner** confesses and entertains.

This issue about "MISTAKES" will be the last time we ask for submissions to adhere to a particular theme. It's been interesting. We've had some journals that soared because of the themes. Early on, our "End of Life in the Age of Technology" struck gold and more recently, last year's "Love, Lust and Longing" heated up the night. What we've found over time is each journal takes on a theme of its own whether we post one or not. Isn't that more fun?

Beginning in 2023, we will no longer charge the mandatory $3 reading fee to submit to *The Ocotillo Review*. Instead, we will provide a tip jar where those who wish to support us can donate what feels right. I hope it works. Please don't carpet bomb us with interplanetary erotica or tasteless political rants. There are places that publish those, but we are not it. This will be a test of our community support. We have faith in the literary community, but we'll do whatever it takes to continue to pay those we publish for their literary art. That is, and will always be, our mission.

I hope you enjoy this issue of *The Ocotillo Review*, "mistakes" and all.

PEACE!

Tony

Perfect Cleavage

As summer's heat moves onto us
my Rocks and Minerals guide tells me
of mica's perfect basal cleavage,
of its paper-thin, flexible sheets of Isinglass, it's called,
heat-proof windows of old stoves and ranges—
of how it's only ever a small layer
of perceived safety
between us and our manufactured
disasters, those coiled and burning snakes.

As summer's heat moves through us
I'm tempted to tell you of finding mica
in the mountain rocks, of how I was six
or maybe seven, peeling those small shimmering sheets,
fingering them in my pocket for luck
against disasters, what else—of how I learned
the splitting cry of a puma,
how our ears perceive it as the pain
of one of our own:
a manufactured human woman on fire.

Montana Agte-Studier

Ask Me Again Tomorrow
Or
The Day Rises from Behind Us

When the moon sets and the streets
are silent, when the sun brings the screaming
birds back to life, when the ocean
inverts and the whales
are beached, all tied
together with seaweed and
fear—then, then in hunger
and hope, the strings
of the puppet are pulled taut
as the tendons in a horse's
neck as it races
toward the white
line of dawn.

- Montana Agte-Studier

Tina is really into samurai movies. Not ninja movies or karate movies or martial arts movies. No, Tina's an aesthete. Mostly Kurosawa. That's canon for Tina. But really any work depicting the feudal system of the Edo period. She's obsessed with the accuracy of props and sets, and shouts at the television when a pompous daimyo flouts a katana instead of the more period-accurate tachi. This is what Tina thinks about all day, just about, instead of thinking about the beans.

The beans are in the backyard next to the limp and rotting tomato plants, somewhere past the burn barrel where we light our trash and sometimes use it to cook s'mores over the open flame, flinching at every little pop and flourish of the flames in case it's a paint can or canister of hairspray.

Doug was on trash-burning duty a week ago, poking styrofoam meal containers from Popeye's deep into the embers, and watching the meal dividers melt into a slime of toxic liquid that disappeared and turned to black smoke when a one-gallon paintcan with the lid tamped down suddenly exploded and shot bits of the rusted barrel into his shins.

Doug waited to see if if the wound'd heal because we don't have the money to go to urgent care in Oak Hill. The wound got infected, and then Doug had to get surgery. The doctors cut out a stretch of gangrenous muscle along his calf and shin.

Tina is Doug's wife, and she's my sister. We all live together on a plot of land about a mile outside Dogsbody. Out here the screech owls holler like drowning women. I have my trailer, and Doug and Tina have theirs, and aside from the five or six half-scrapped cars rowed up along the gravel-and-mud drive (and fuck you if you think that's a stereotype), there's not much else out here.

I say all that because I don't really blame Tina for what she did after that.

See, the reason we got Popeye's that night was because our Uncle Gary won the lottery and gave us each ten thousand dollars to do like we wished. Gary won the Powerball four days before the paint can exploded, and after it happened, and after Doug's leg got infected, and after Doug had to have surgery to remove part of his calf muscle and spent three days just being "monitored," which is what Doug calls "picking your pocket after the deed is done," Tina went back to Uncle Gary to ask if she could have the full amount for the hospital bill, which she figured was a hell of a lot more than ten thousand.

Gary told her, "I'm giving you ten thousand, like everybody else, and if you don't like it, you can fuck off."

So, she took it. Of course she did. And the first thing she did was buy a brand new laptop and pay up on some high-speed internet for a full two years, and then buy herself a subscription to the Criterion Collection of Asian Cinema.

"I didn't know you even liked them Jap movies," Doug said from his hospital bed, even though he had a doctor who was of Japanese descent, and I had to explain to the man that that was just what Doug's Pa called all Asian people because he didn't know any Asian people except the ones he'd fought back in the Pacific. The doctor didn't look too impressed, but he didn't look too put out either, like he was used to the occasional hillbilly coming in and needing his expertise and paying him back with nothing but ignorant slurs.

The second thing Tina did was go to the billing office at the hospital and ask them point blank how much they really did owe for Doug's stay in the hospital and for the services of his Asian doctor, to which the woman behind the partitioned glass at the billing office said, "You don't have to call him Asian. He's just a doctor. And the bill is $176,453.47."

So Tina, who had the ten thousand for Doug intact, and what was left of her own ten thousand, which was around six after she'd got done spending it on the computer and the internet and the movies, didn't even ask me for my ten thousand because it didn't make much difference in the face of all that debt, which was a relief to me but a heartache to her, and she took that sixteen thousand of her and Doug's and went across the county line to the riverboat casino and played the roulette wheel in that bold way that people who've lived all their lives without money can play.

People with money can't imagine why poor people do some of the dumb shit we do, but when you got nothing, sometimes shooting for everything is more appealing than dragging out your low-grade happiness in dribs and drabs. We know chances aren't good we'll hold onto any money, so we're a little reckless, and sometimes that kind of foolhardy behavior pays off in a place like a riverboat casino.

Tina won $96,000, which brought her grand total to $112,000, give or take a few bucks, and we celebrated that night by getting drunk as skunks off wine that cost forty dollars a bottle, which was about the most expensive thing we'd ever poured down our throats by a long shot. All the while Doug was still laid up in the hospital, and when we woke the next morning we were late to check him out, and he was in front of the hospital in a wheelchair looking sour.

So on the drive back to our respective trailers, Tina gets this half-cocked smile on her face and taps the steering wheel with the only press-on nail she had left (somewhere in the wine-drunk night she'd lost the other nine to mishap and misadventure) and said, "Guess what?"

And Doug, who was feeling disgusted with his hacked-up leg in the back seat and depressed for being forgotten and made to wait, and with his pain pills wearing off, said, "I s'pose you're going to tell me whether or not I ask for it."

And Tina told him how she'd already made more than half the bill—"I'm good at that spinning wheel. I might just become a professional gambler."

To which Doug said it didn't work like that, that you couldn't play roulette professionally, and she had to pick a game like Texas Hold'em or learn to count cards for Black Jack, but Tina wasn't deterred and just kept smiling and tapping that one pink nail beglittered in rhinestones—and told him how she already had a plan for making up the remainder.

"How's that?" Doug said.

I turned to her, too, because this was the first I'd heard of a plan. I'd just been waiting for her to tell Doug about the $112 K.

And she said, "After I won all that money, I met a doctor at the riverboat."

I had the faint memory of a slim man in a nice suit with thinning hair, in his fifties maybe, too old for Tina but debonair, like he'd stepped out of one of those New Yorker cartoons you see in pop-up ads, a snooty butler with a pencil-dark moustache. That kind of refinement was the kind of thing Tina had always gone for, or would have if she'd ever known a guy with that kind of refinement.

And that's also when I had a memory of us getting drunk on the wine, and the man joining us and congratulating us, and us asking him if he wanted to hang with us in our booth, and I'd seen then that Tina was thinking about sleeping with the man, and I made a magnanimous decision to, as her brother, let her have this one indiscretion because, frankly, Doug wasn't all that much to look at, and it had been his fault for standing so close to the burn barrel anyway, and I got to wishing I had a woman who'd be impressed that my sister just won a hundred thousand dollars. I wished this imaginary woman might sleep with me, but all I could find when I made a round of the casino were a few bleary-looking, blue-haired retirees dressed up for a night out in 1958.

When I got back to the booth, Tina and the man were gone, and I said out loud to my drunken self, "Good for her. Good for her," and then went and passed out on the shore right beside the river boat, smelling the swamp-muck scent of seaweed and diesel and the food remains slicked upon the fetid plastic trash, and in the morning I wandered up to my room in the hotel and stole a towel and a few wash cloths and shoved them under my shirt, and then Tina was in the hallway, looking shy like we had a secret, and I understood that it wasn't because she'd slept with the New Yorker butler-man, or at least it wasn't only that, but I didn't ask her what else might have happened. Now, in the car, I wished I had.

"The doctor gentleman we met last night gave me these," she said, and held out three gel capsules a murky yellow that looked like the kind you'd take for hay fever every four hours.

"What the hell are those?" Doug asked.

"Revolutionary drugs," she said.

"And they're for me? To fix my leg?" Doug asked.

She laughed, a bright snort that rolled up the hood of the car and came back down in the back seat and hit Doug like a slap. "No, stupid," she said. "They're to sell. They're worth a hundred thousand a piece, and this doctor sold them to me for a third of that."

The feeling in my stomach turned electric, then icy, then like a ball of barbed wire tumbling down through my intestines, and I rolled down the window and sicked all down the door panel.

"You're hosing that off before it peels the paint," Tina said, and stopped at the next service station and asked if they had a spigot, and they pointed her to the back, and I hosed it down with water while she and Doug talked in the car for a bit. While I stood there with the water gushing out, they got more animated until their voices pulsed out the windows, and then Tina was out, and they were yelling back and forth in the open air, and Tina was backing up further and further until she was almost to the pumps, like the force of their anger was repelling them from one another like very strong magnets, and I was glad I wasn't between them and that I had a task, watching the wine-dark vomit dribble off the car door and roll across the concrete into a rusty drain.

They cooled down enough to drive home in rageful quiet, but as soon as we hit the property, Doug was back at it.

"He sold you magic beans, Tina! Ya dumb whore!"

To which Tina, who was used to such terrible name-calling, shot back, "It's a nano-technological, non-invasive treatement for cancer, like I told you, ya fucking moron!"

The way she said all that, I could imagine the butler man repeating those medical phrases to her all night, making her memorize and believe in them—so much blind faith she'd be willing to hock a hundred thousand dollars for three little plastic gel caps—and I could see her needing to believe, and that's when I knew I'd failed her as a brother, failed to watch out for all the people that meant to take things from her and turn her life to shit, the way Doug had done.

And when we got home, I failed again—I was too slow—to stop Doug grabbing the three pills out of her hand, howling, "Magic beans! Magic fucking beans!" and limping out to the backyard, and throwing them past the burn barrel, the sight of his own misfortune and shame, where they landed somewhere among the dirt and weeds and were lost to the bugs and roots and singed bramble lacing the ground.

I heard Tina that night crying and then not crying, and for a while I thought she'd left, but when I went over to her and Doug's trailer, hoping to cool things off between them, there was Doug on the bed in their shoddy bedroom with the missing panels on the walls moaning for more codeine while Tina turned up the volume on her new laptop so the gruff voice of Toshiro Mifune shouted Doug down into oblivion. I saw how Tina liked those movies, because she has the spirit of a samurai, and either she's going to make good on her ferocity or plunge her life headlong into a ritual sepukku the way so many samurai and so many women in Dogsbody, Ohio have done since time immemorial, giving up their bodies and their good years and their energies to failed attempts at glory.

And the tense equilibrium that's ensued since that morning is a welcome quiet—they don't shout anymore, the way they used to—but also something new, like something has to happen next, like it can't go on this way with us waiting like two samurai in a field of softly rustling wheat with swords held high, awaiting the inevitable swift end.

When I think about that, I think it's my time to make something happen. Maybe all it takes is one move, one strike, which is maybe what Tina has known all along and why she took such a stupid, glorious, wonderful, asinine chance.

"We'll make it right," I said to her just this morning after poking my head in to see her and Doug still there in their respective misery, like they never sleep anymore, one waiting for the codeine to take hold before going down into that cottony stupor again, and the other deep in research of a distant period in the distant land of Nippon, dreaming of a past that has nothing to do with her but must hold something in its

8

unintelligible and courtly subtexts, a place where all the unspoken signs and alien customs mean something more.

I walked out to the backyard then, thinking maybe I'd look for those pills. Or those beans. Whatever you want to call them. Pick your dream: a fairy tale, a science-fiction. Sometimes the ways we dream don't mean as much as the fact that we do still dream. And I have to admit, that tomato plant, the dead and rotting one—it's looking healthy again.

- D. Michael Armstrong

Coming soon! The following poem is from *The Flowers of Nonchalance* by **Dan Smart** due out fall of 2022

FIDDLE

There are things that are important
beyond all this fiddle.
-Marianne Moore

The truth is
that art isn't
worth all that much.

The laundry is
far more important
than poetry;

a picture's 1000
word minimum
is short work for autofill.

But still,
there is something
beyond pleasure

in the slightest accord
between violin strings.
It's in the way

the whole thing shimmers
where its parts
made no difference,

or else strained
in imitation;
the way a lack

of explanation
satisfies our yearning
for inconsequence.

A poem has no instructions,
but once read,
achieves summation—

a baby's cry
means nothing, but delivers
consolation.

"Do you like the stripes or the flowers?" I hold up two sets of sheets as my stepmother and I stand in the home goods section of Target.

Joy stares at both. "The flowers."

"Okay, pink or the blue?" I put the striped sheets back on the shelf and grab another set with blue flowers.

"But we don't know what size to get."

"Dad told me what to get. Queen."

My dad had recently decided that my stepmother's dementia had progressed to the point where he could no longer take care of her at home, so he'd rented an apartment in a senior living center. The apartment's bedroom was smaller than the one at home, so they were having to downsize from a king- to a queen-sized bed, and he'd sent me with Joy and his credit card to buy new sheets.

Joy stares at me, trying to decide if she knows me.

"Richard," I say, "Richard told me."

"Oh, okay."

"So which is it, pink or blue?"

She puts her finger to her chin as she considers the choice.

"Blue," she pauses, "but we don't know what size to get."

* * *

My parents had divorced during the summer between my fifth and sixth grade years, and my mother and I had left San Angelo, moving ninety miles away to Abilene. I was a daddy's girl, so I lived for my every-other-weekend trip on the Greyhound back to San Angelo to see my dad. When I arrived on Friday nights, he'd make tacos for dinner, and we'd eat them as we watched TV. On Saturday mornings, I'd go with him to work at the grocery store, and then, after lunch at McDonald's, he'd drop me off at his apartment where I'd spend the afternoon watching television or listening to his Creedence Clearwater

Revival eight-track. He also had Neil Diamond, but I wasn't a fan. After work, he'd pick me up and we'd go to Shakey's Pizza for dinner and then to a movie. On Sunday mornings, he'd feed me a bowl of Fruit Loops before putting me back on the bus.

One Saturday morning as I was sitting in the break room at the grocery store, thumbing through a magazine, one of the assistant managers came in for a cup of coffee.

"Your daddy needs to find a girlfriend." She poured the dregs of the carafe into her cup. "It's not good for him to go home to an empty apartment every night. He drinks too much."

I knew exactly what "drinks too much" meant. One Saturday morning, after sleeping over at my best friend's house, we'd gone outside to play and found her father sprawled in the front yard. My friend returned to the back door and yelled, "Mama, Daddy's out here. Looks like he drank too much."

That night I told my dad that I wished he had a girlfriend. I'm not sure if he'd already started dating on our off weekends or whether he decided to take the advice of an eleven-year-old, but during my next visit, he introduced me to Carolyn.

Carolyn was younger than my dad and definitely out of his league. She also had a daughter, a chunky toddler with blond ringlets. They joined us for our usual Saturday lunch at McDonald's, and afterward, my dad sent me off to spend the afternoon with Carolyn and her daughter while he finished his shift. We stopped at Woolworth's for a bottle of nail polish, and back at her apartment, Carolyn painted my fingernails black.

I hoped my dad would marry Carolyn, but the next time I visited, he didn't even mention her.

* * *

A few months later, he announced that he wanted to introduce me to his new girlfriend, Joy. Instead of our usual Saturday night dinner at Shakey's, he took me to meet Joy at Twin Mountains Steak House, so I knew it was serious. Joy wasn't as young or pretty as Carolyn, but she drove a green Camaro, which I assumed meant she was cool. The next time I returned to San Angelo, it was to attend my dad and Joy's wedding in the chapel of the Methodist church. After the ceremony, we returned to Joy's house, which was now also my dad's house.

"This will be your room." He set my bag in what appeared to be a guest room.

I was excited about having two bedrooms, one at my mother's house and another at my dad's, so as soon as I returned home on Sunday afternoon, I pulled out the Sears catalog. I finally decided on a set of sheets and a matching bedspread with hot pink daisies, tore out the pages, and mailed them to my dad. I would save my allowance so that the next time I went to San Angelo, I could get my dad to take me to K-Mart to buy a bulletin board and maybe a Donny Osmond poster to hang in my new room. When I returned for my next visit, however, the guest room was exactly the same. Same threadbare sheets, same antique bedspread covered in yellow roses. My room at my dad's remained the perfect guest room for an old lady, with nothing that belonged to me other than the suitcase I brought with me each visit.

What did change was how I spent my weekends in San Angelo.

"Why don't we go see a movie?" my dad would suggest, and I'd chime in with the name of whatever new release I hadn't yet seen.

"I don't want to go to the movie," Joy shook her head, "They're just not as good as they used to be."

"Then why don't we go out to dinner?"

"Hon, I'm making spaghetti." Now Joy was annoyed.

Turns out that green Camaro did not mean Joy was cool. Instead, she was a homebody who, after working all week, just wanted to spend her weekends reading. No McDonald's burgers or Shakey's pizza and, definitely, no movies. Instead, I sat on the couch, watching whatever lame television shows the networks aired on Friday and Saturday nights while Joy read silently on the end of the couch and my dad snoozed in his recliner.

If the weekends were miserable, the week at Christmas and the two weeks in the summer were unbearable. My stepbrother, Don, who was Joy's youngest and only child still
14

at home, controlled the television during the day while my dad and Joy were at work. In my memory, he watched *Gilligan's Island* all day, but I know that can't have been true because none of the three networks would have tied up an entire day with a marathon of *Gilligan's Island* episodes.

With nothing else to do, I borrowed books from Joy's shelves. She was a member of the Book of the Month Club and so had the bloody thrillers and steamy romances I didn't have access to at the school library. After a while, though, even reading became boring, and soon I was looking for reasons to skip weekends altogether and cut my school vacation visits short. Stacy's birthday party, a volleyball tournament, a church choir concert.

* * *

As I grew distant from my dad, he grew close to Joy's family. He became a stand-in for Don's mostly absent father, teaching him to shave and the importance of changing the oil in his car. He became the grandfather to my older stepsiblings' children, building them a playhouse in the backyard and taking them for ice cream. On the rare occasion I found myself in San Angelo for Thanksgiving, we'd go to Joy's parents' house, where my dad was clearly a beloved member of the clan, playing dominoes and watching football, while I sat awkwardly in the corner, counting the minutes until it was time to go home. At the same time my dad became a member of Joy's family, I became a member of my stepfather's family. Jerry taught me to shoot a basketball and the importance of flying the flag on holidays. I became a sister to his children, an aunt to his grandchildren. Every Christmas Eve, I watched White Christmas with my step-siblings while we ate pecan pie. On Christmas morning, we put gag gifts in the bottoms of each others' stockings.

I often wonder if things would've been different if my dad had ordered that bedding from Sears or if he'd ever told Joy we were going to the movies without her. While he missed the little opportunities, he never failed to show up for the big events of my life, and he never stopped trying to include me in the big events of his. I was an adult before I understood he had done his best to navigate the blending of his old family with his new one, filling the hole that my mother had created when she left and took me with her.

* * *

Several years ago, I asked my dad what it had been like to become a stepfather.

"Well," It was how he began most of his answers to my questions. "I knew I couldn't take their dad's place, and I didn't want to, so I just tried to make a place of my own in their lives. I think I was pretty successful."

My dad's response got me thinking about my relationship with Joy. She'd been at my dad's side at my graduations and wedding, and they were there together the day after my son was born, but had she made a place of her own in my life? If suddenly Joy had been removed from the picture, my dad's relationships with her family would have stayed pretty much the same. He would have continued inviting my stepbrothers over for lunch on Wednesdays and gone to all the grandson's soccer games. He would have babysat the great-grandkids or made a rocking chair without hesitation if asked.

But what would have happened to me and Joy if my dad had disappeared? Would we have continued talking on the phone each week? Would I have sent flowers for Mother's Day? Would she have sent me a card with a thirty-five dollar check on my birthday?

I decided it was time to let go of my childhood resentments and to try to make a place for myself in Joy's life. When I called, instead of letting her immediately get my dad on the phone, I'd say, "Wait, first I want to talk to you." I began sharing my favorite books and jigsaw puzzles with her. During their last Christmas visit, I got the ingredients so we could decorate Christmas cookies together. It was during that visit I noticed her memory slipping.

One afternoon I asked my dad to make a grocery store run with me.

"I think something's wrong with Joy," I said, "She keeps repeating herself."

"Yeah, she's been forgetting stuff lately." He shrugged.

"I think you should talk to her doctor."

In January, my stepbrother and I threw a surprise birthday

16

party for my dad's 80th birthday, and despite that fact that I and all three of Joy's children had talked to her several times about the plan, she was the most surprised person in the room when she and my dad walked into the restaurant.

Clearly something was wrong, and so my dad talked her into a rare visit to the doctor, which was quickly followed with a diagnosis of dementia. I knew whatever chance I'd had to build a relationship with her had passed and wondered if my meager efforts had had any effect at all. I learned the answer to that question the day before I took Joy shopping for bedding. I was packing up my dad's books in the front room when I overheard the cleaning lady talking to Joy in the kitchen.

"So, is that your daughter helping you pack?"

"Who?" Joy was confused.

"Packing the books in there. Is that your daughter?"

Joy looked around the corner. "Oh, no, that's Richard's daughter."

"So I guess that makes her your daughter too." The woman laughed.

"No. That's Richard's daughter."

Yes, I'd waited too long.

* * *

"Blue flowers it is," I toss the sheets into the cart. "And look, there's a matching bedspread! Like it?" I hold it above the cart.

"Yes, I do, but are we sure it's the right size?"

"Yep, Richard told me the new bed is a queen. Let's get the whole set." I dropped the comforter into the cart.

Joy smiled and placed her hand on my arm. "I can't believe that just as we got to be good friends, I'm moving away."

"I know." I patted her hand. "I can't believe it either." I gave her hand a squeeze and she pulled it away, once again confused about who I was and why I had tears in my eyes.

"I think that's everything we need." I began pushing the cart up the aisle, headed for the checkout, Joy following a step behind me.

"But are you sure we got the right size?"

- Karen Collier

Pantoum for Fishermen (1900)

All must share *the right to fish the tide*
about the mouth of Ketchiken Creek.
No one owns *the tidal ebb and flow*
so all *must spread their nets in turn.*

About the mouth of Ketchiken Creek
salmon fill the water with their silver.
All fishermen *must spread their nets in turn*
along the *Tongass Narrows at high-water mark.*

As salmon filled the water with their silver,
the ancestral *right of passage to deep waters*
along the *Tongass Narrows at high water mark*
was blocked by Heckman's *seines 150 fathoms long.*

The ancestral *right of passage to deep waters*
will not be cast aside by Judge Brown's court.
When Heckman blocked the channel with his nets,
he knew he would catch *quarrels, even bloodshed.*

Common decency will not be cast aside by Judge Brown's court.
Ketchiken Creek should run with salmon, not with blood.
Heckman's selfishness risked *quarrels, even bloodshed.*
What couldn't he understand? Say it again:

The creek should run with salmon, not with blood.
Heckman doesn't own *the tide that ebbs and flows.*
Now the court will make him understand
that fair men share *the right to fish the tide.*

(All italicized phrases are adapted from Sutter v. Heckman,
1 Alaska Rpts. 81 (D.Ct. Alaska 1900).)

- Stan Crawford

"Oscar," Miguel said more than asked.

"Yes, sir," I said, looking up from the bilingual questionnaire for my uncle's newest workman's comp client.

"I'm going to need you to go on a little drive for me."

"No *problemo*," I said, trying not to betray my enthusiasm. We'd commuted that day from Fort Collins to Greeley, a blue-collar town about a forty-five minute drive through industrial farm and cattle country, in his new Italian roadster, an Alfa Romeo. I was chomping at the bit to open it up on the wide open country highways crisscrossing the plains rolling out east of the Rockies. It didn't have the pickup of his Porsche, which I'd gotten up to one twenty the week before, but the sleek design of the silver, bullet-shaped convertible more than made up for any lack of horsepower.

"And scrap that last invoice from *Menudo*'s case."

"*Por que,* boss?"

Menudo was a 1980s Puerto Rican boy band that introduced us to the likes of Ricky Martin and the crossover hit, "*Subete a Mi Moto*"/"Ride My Motorcycle." It was also the nickname one of the paralegals gave Javier Lopez when we passed around the photo of the guy's mangled, helmetless scalp.

"There's a new one with your courier fee in the printer."

Menudo and his Harley were run off the road by a white woman whose insurance policy maxed out a $50,000 payout for any potential negligence on her part. And considering his client lost not only his chosen mode of transportation, but that he'd likely be in some sort of physical discomfort for the foreseeable future, Miguel wanted to make sure the poor schmo got his hands on that dough before the doctors, nurses, and physical therapists claimed the lion's share. Never mind the firm's 33% plus my $120 surcharge to drive halfway to Denver, meet an insurance agent on the side of I-76, sign a release and then meet the gang at a bar and grill back in Greeley, a cashier's check for fifty large in hand.

* * *

One weekend afternoon, for a lack of anything better to do, I cruised Fort Collins in the drop-top in search of two things beyond the dollar menu at the Wendy's drive-thru: first and foremost were the hotties orbiting the red brick buildings of the Colorado State campus, where I gleaned more than a couple of lusty leers to give my ego some quick, if fleeting, boosts; and secondly, just for kicks, to see if I could spot any black people in this lily-white college town of a hundred thousand. In two hours, I burned a quarter tank of gas and saw but one—a young, skinny black man who disappeared into an Appleby's. And besides myself, Miguel, or Alice, who you'd assume was white if you missed the Dr. Martinez-Martinez moniker; there wasn't much *raza* either.

So imagine my surprise the first time we rolled into Greeley, a town with over a third of its population composed of non-white *Latinos* living off all the work white people don't wanna do. And much like my old neighborhood back in Texas, it was as if old Mexico never really left, but merely changed names from places like Guadalupe or San Jacinto to places like Greeley or Houston, towns that kept their migrant farmers and meat processors, folks who actually put food on American tables at less than a reasonable price—and at no small risk to their physical or mental well-being.

> *Go north,*
> *Brown man.*
>
> *Find work.*
> *Brown woman.*
>
> *In it but for la familia,*
> *La Virgen y El Tri.*
>
> *But remember,*
> *The road is,*

As always,
Is full of holes,

The holes,
Full of snakes.

Sooner or later, while working to pay down a mortgage, or to send money back home, or both, he or she is likely enough to fall, and who better to help them back on their feet than the bilingual Attorney at Law, Miguel Martinez—their guide through the legal labyrinth of workman's comp, a tedious, time-consuming process that helps keep the firm's lights on but hardly puts a dent in Miguel's penchant for fancy cars and Jamaican vacations.

That kind of booty comes from P.I. windfalls like *Menudo*'s or high-dollar fees collected from criminals dumb or unlucky enough to get caught with their hands in the proverbial cookie jar.

* * *

The alleged perpetrator is a 6'2" light-skinned Mexican national with a thick Freddy Fender mustache and a bowl-cut mullet of wiry black hair that reaches down to the middle of his hulky back. His bleary, bloodshot eyes point alternately at the table, floor and judge. If he pleads out, four to eight with good behavior, twice that if found guilty a second time for felony possession of over an ounce of coke with intent to distribute, a bum deal any which way the father of two tries to cut that shit.

"Do you understand the terms of the plea you have entered here today, Mr. Garcia?" the judge says.

Miguel nods for his client to lean down so he can translate the perfunctory question.

The big *Mestizo* nods and whispers, "*Si.*"

"He does, Your Honor."

"And that you are making this plea of your own free will."

Lawyer and client repeat the pantomime.

"He does, Your Honor."

And soon enough, the white judge asks the black bailiff—only the second African American I'd seen in over a month—to re-cuff and lead the truly humbled immigrant to his prolonged if immediate fate.

* * *

"I'll be back tomorrow," I said to Dallas, an undergraduate skate-punk busy stirring the mushroom tea on the agenda that day.

"Sweet," he said to either my words or his concoction.

"And maybe we go snowboarding the next day."

"Perfect," he said, blowing on a spoonful of the psychedelic.

"Dallas?"

"What? Oh, right," he said, "snowboarding."

"Yeah," I said, feeling less and less connected to yet another posse of rich white kids—this particular posse from up around the DFW metroplex by way of Austin. "Maybe hit El Dora in a couple of days."

"Watch out for Bambi," he said with a chuckle.

A few nights before, we were driving up through the southern Rockies, in a pretty heavy snow that did little to slow the 60-70 mph traffic, when a huge buck split the hundred yards between the flatbed in front of my Accord's knee-high bumper, then cleared the barricade to the other side of the mountain-carving interstate. A second later and we would have surely clipped the beast and absorbed 400 pounds of pure muscle, bone, and antler through the windshield.

"No shit," I said, echoing his laugh as I opened the front door. "Laters."

"See ya when I see ya," he said and added more sugar to the elixir.

* * *

With the front having blown through, the drive north was overcast but much less foreboding, so I threw on my headphones, turned on some grunge anthem full blast and, like the dumbest Mexican this side of the Pecos, drove right past a Colorado State Trooper—also headed north on I-25—with expired Texas plates, a Bob Marley sticker on my back windshield and an ounce of high-grade shwag I'd scored for Miguel in Boulder.

* * *

"Now reach over with your left hand," instructs the officer from behind my car on the passenger side, "and open your glove compartment with your left hand, making sure to keep your right hand up and visible as you do it."

"Yes sir," I say in shock at both the circumstance and my utter stupidity, remembering the standard operating procedure for a cross-country mule—a little under the radar commerce, often in an older model vehicle that doubles as payment for any and all the risk incurred along the way.

I reach over and do as instructed.

No way he doesn't find it.

It's hidden pretty good.

It isn't.

He's looking for more and might miss it.

No way.

"Now, is there anything in there I should know about?" he asks.

"Just my proof of insurance, sir."

"Ok, reach in there and grab it and then sit up and put your hands on the wheel until I get over to your side of the vehicle."

"Yes sir, Officer."

No fucking way!

He opens the door with his left hand, his right one on his gun, the holster unclipped.

"Do you have any identification?"

I open my wallet, pull out a tattered folded-up print-out of an expired temporary driver's license and my proof of insurance, also expired.

He takes my paperwork and says, "Now, Mr. Rodriguez, please step out and move to the back of the vehicle."

23

"Yes sir," I say and take a quick inventory of the ro-
tund, barrel-chested gringo. He's maybe five years older than
me and a couple of inches taller with a thin brown mustache
and short, side-parted hair.

He looks slow and soft in the middle but sturdy. Maybe he played tackle or guard in high school...maybe even
some college ball...

*You could outrun him like that mojado Mom picked up
'til the border patrol chased him into the desert. Man he was
fast...*

The cold northerly shoves me south toward old Mexico, the trunk, and certain doom.

"Where are you headed today?"

"Fort Collins, to visit my uncle, a lawyer," I say, sure to
mention my affiliation with his line of work, even as I struggle
to make eye contact.

"And where are you coming from?"

"Boulder."

"But your plates say Texas?"

"A friend and I drove in from Austin a few days ago."

"That so?"

"Yes, sir."

"And where's your friend now?"

"Back in Boulder, with our old roommate from UT."

"I see," he says, unconvinced. "And are you transport-
ing any guns, drugs or any other contraband today?"

"No sir," I say, failing again to hide the warble in my
voice.

"And tell me again why you're headed to Fort Collins?"

"To visit my uncle, Miguel Martinez, who I used to
clerk for," I say, doubling down on my only card.

"Why?"

"Well, it *is* the holidays."

"Hey, buddy," he says, pinning my squirrelly eyes
down for a moment, "I'm the one asking questions here."

"Yes, sir, Officer," I apologize, "We're supposed to ex-
change gifts and such. You know?"

24

"I *do*," he says, glancing at the Rasta king's sticker. "But would you mind if I take a quick look anyway?"

I look down at the pavement, then up at the hay-colored plains extending east...*Run, wetback! Run!...*then back up to his small, brown eyes and say, "Sure. Why not?"

"Good," he says with a cold smile.

Fucking pig...

"Then follow me to my cruiser."

Godamnmotherfuck!!!

He opens his passenger side door and pulls out a clipboard, attaches a form and fills in the first few lines.

Don't do it, dumbass!

He offers it to me along with his black pen.

I don't take it, and ask, "What happens if I don't sign that?"

"Now, Mr. Rodriguez," he says, his stern look tightening the reins on the reality of the situation, "it's obvious to me that you're hiding something."

"I'm not though."

"Come on, man. You can't even look me in the eyes."

"That's 'cause cops make me nervous," I say, again looking for comfort in the truth.

"And you're sure that's all it is?"

"That is all it is!"

"Then why won't you let me look? You know, for my own peace of mind."

"Because," I say, my pupils locking onto his for the first time, "I don't think it's necessary."

"Is that so?" he says, a bit taken aback, almost impressed.

"Yes, sir," I say, the quiver in my voice completely gone. "It is."

"Well, Mr. Rodriguez," he says, his incredulous smile thawing as his beady brown eyes shoot from the clipboard to the passing cars to the jagged mountain wall that shadows the interstate all the way from Denver to Wyoming, and beyond, "then I guess you'll be on your way."

"Are you serious?"

"Yes, sir," he says with a nod. "Just go sit in your car and I'll be up there in a few minutes."

"Yes, sir. Thank you, sir," I say, and soon enough sign a couple of warning tickets for driving with headphones and expired tags.

I roll up the window and watch him walk back to his cruiser.

Not even a no insurance ticket!

"That's right, motherfucker," I say with a snicker. "Sic Miguel on your ass."

* * *

It took an extra day to get back to Houston because I went to Midway instead of O'Hare.

Of course there's two airports in Chi-town, pendejo! It's a major fucking city!

By the time I got to baggage claim, I caught the first hints of the hundred-degree tidal wave of humidity awaiting me out on the barely-shaded sidewalk for arrivals flying into Hobby on Southwest Airlines that day.

Mom was of course late, so I sat on my luggage and stewed in the cauldron of the town where I'd spent the first twenty years of my life, before escaping to Austin and then all points north—well, Kansas, Colorado, and this last time, Chicago—until flying back home with very little idea how to use a seemingly worthless English degree to help navigate the next year of my nascent adulthood, not to mention the rest of my life.

Law school?
Fuck that.
Then what?
Miguel's got that new practice in Colorado Springs…
Paul's in…money in the bank…just cost you your soul…
Fuck! That!
Then, what?

Mom pulled up in her year-old Chevy pick-up, the new truck sheen marred by the countless workers, tools, and bags of concrete it had transported.

26

"*Hola Toti!*" she said, trying to sound happy but not pulling it off.

"Hi, Mom," I said, failing at the same subterfuge.

"Good to see you!"

"You too!"

"Thanks for coming to get me."

"No problem," she said, driving away from the outdated airport. "But I thought you were supposed to stay through the summer?"

"I couldn't get enough work and didn't really want to, once I realized how fucking cold it gets up there."

"I know."

"And my new friend, that guy I told you about, has a room I can rent up in Austin for a month or so."

"A month?" she asked, turning onto I-45 North toward The Brisket House, where we always ate whenever back by the barrio.

"Yeah, while I look for my own place I guess."

"You could stay here," she said, her voice cracking as she continued her proposition, "and work for me."

"Doing construction?" I said defensively. "Yeah, that's why I went to college, to break my back like *Tio* Manuel…"

"Especially," she cut me off, oblivious to my words as her tears began to flow, "since I just gave away my little *Lupita*."

"Excuse me, what?!"

"Miguel just came and took her away from me!" she cried.

I groaned. I'd heard that a short *Mestiza* who had added one too many mouths to her litter had laid her burden down at my mother's doorstep. Mom—Rosa Maria Martinez Anom—was a woman of means—first as the owner of a record store; then a Mexican sporting goods store named after me; then a *Tejano* bar where *Flaco Jimenez* once turned up to play an impromptu set; and then finally, for over twenty years, a concrete contractor unafraid to mix it up with the good old boys, laying slab after slab of cement over the swamp that once was the Bayou City.

But her work kept her busy from morning till night,

and her other son, my little brother Steve, already felt the lack of her time and attention. I knew more than anyone that my mother was a woman who was always better at bringing home the bacon than cooking it.

"You mean to tell me you took that baby?"

"Didn't I just tell you that Miguel did?" she said, lashing out.

"Yeah, but from you?"

She nodded and sobbed as she exited the highway.

"Are you serious?"

"*Pero esa mujer me la dio!*" she pleaded to me, God, the universe—anyone that would listen…

"Okay, she gave her to you, but you said I was right! That Steve still needs you! That you still have a lot of work to do there."

My condescension, the almost inevitable karma of parenthood, had to sting, but I couldn't, wouldn't let up—for my little brother *and* that little girl…and for my own selfish ass.

"You owe that boy!" I barked as she pulled into the parking lot.

"Don't tell me what I know!"

"Then why did you take her?"

"I couldn't help it!" she cried and threw the truck into Park, resting her world-weary head on the steering wheel.

I looked up at the rustic two-story restaurant, my stomach gnawing on itself so that any sympathy, let alone empathy, was hard to muster.

"And what the fuck does Miguel have to do with it anyway?"

"*Pues,*" she said, looking over at me, eyes sad as ever, "*tu tia.*"

Tu tia. If I could count the number of times she had said those two words, *tu tia,* when I asked her what was wrong…*your aunt.*

My aunt, her own sister Juana, a death knell—like at that Christmas party when Georgie spiderwebbed our windshield as we tried to extricate ourselves from his mom's psy-

28

chotic tendrils; and that time she ratted Mom's construction company out to the I.R.S. because *Abuela* had chosen to live with Mom instead of her most sociopathic spawn.

Juana, in it for the Social Security, her Florida fortune having gone down the Texas crapper. And then, of course, when she heard that someone had given her sister the daughter she had always wanted.

Looking at Mom, her head still resting on the steering wheel, I thought that she suddenly looked older. And more tired than ever.

She had given me life, and had worked tirelessly to build a life for me and for my brother. But, in my not so humble opinion, she was ill-equipped to give that complex little miracle the tools with which to succeed—not just in the acquisition of wealth, but to actually grow into a well-rounded adult who can not only wipe her own butt and pay her own bills, but get along with others and have a good grasp on her motivations, so as to better regulate her emotions without all the mechanisms we Americans tend to abuse—drugs, religion, sports, media, each other—when the going gets too rough or too boring or too fill-in-the-blank for us to make good sense of...* * *

"If you take that girl," I warn as she drops me off at Bush Intercontinental, "it will be at my little brother's expense."

"I know," she says.

"And he'll make you pay."

"I know."

"You'll be buying him one thing after another to fill the hole that you and that piece of shit Enzo failed to fill."

She nods as if she's actually listening, as if she could somehow stop herself from accepting such a universal gift any more than our crazy aunt could stop herself from sabotaging her sister by calling my miserable uncle up in Colorado; or any more than that uncle could stop himself from jumping on the first flight to Houston to whisk that little brown bundle of love and diapers back up north, to a life unfathomably more secure than the one waiting in the extended cab of Mom's truck.

* * *

In the end, it was easy to picture Miguel on bended knee, begging his more selfless sister to breathe hope into his lifeless, if luxurious home, especially with no progeny to help rationalize such material excess.

And it was even easier to see Mom giving up her heart's desire so that her baby brother might not freeze to death, up in that cold, red state.

- Oscar Rodriguez

INOCULATIONS

Something oily in the water. Restless
regiments, thunderheads beyond
the mountains. The child next door
has stopped singing.

Since noon I'm trying to recall that thing I know
we keep forgetting in the forest. I'm desperate
to determine whether steel or basalt
is the harder matter.

Under an overhanging shelf of mud and roots,
you and I have dug our fingers into veins
of stone, tangled our hair with the tree's
blind tendrils.

I hear you singing, loudly, to inoculate my fears.
You are telling me not to worry. That the mosses
lay down their spongy carpets over the earth's
abrasions. That lichens live a thousand years

and steel can be burned to shine like an exploding
star. You say we are already in the green belly
of the forest, that there can be a heart outside
the body. And I know these things.

But I also know a fingernail will scrape and scrape
and then break off ragged, bloody. And while
you keep scratching the hard-packed earth
with your song, next door there is no singing.

- Karen McPherson

Wildlife of the Party

I:
To Live On Air

There are some things I don't really want to see or hear or do. Glass jars of things that live inside me. How many bleary times have I opened a lid and added salt instead of sugar to a pie or cake recipe? How many times have I said the wrong thing to someone, instantly regretting the insistence of my flippant remark, about someone's clothes or hair or teeth? How do I revise myself while watching my errors orbiting the earth again and again like some personal satellite that is more like a space station?

I wasn't terribly desultory or slinky in my youth, but I did have several memorable party or bar encounters. With a smirk I once poured a beer over a coworker's head at a Missoula, Montana bar. He'd made a remark, which I have forgotten, but it made me angry. This was the same drunken man who, unharmed, drove his truck off a small bridge one night and another time spent the night passed out beneath the coat rack at an office party.

We drank a lot in Montana, although I should just speak for myself. I was proud of drinking more shots than men much larger than me. I thought I drove my car better when I was inebriated. I had blackouts and couldn't remember anything. At one MFA party one of my teachers kissed my best friend, who was on his lap, and told everyone standing nearby to exit the room. In college I liked shots of tequila because it seemed somewhere between alcohol and a drug. At a dorm party some guy I didn't know crept his fingers up my pants leg while we sat on a sofa. "You were so cool about it," some other guy said to frozen me. That remark was like seeing only part of a person. I was usually quiet and shy, with too much beneath my surface.

All drunks are discontented and surrounded by too much gravity. Neighbors metamorphosize into silhouettes at windows, shadows at doorsteps, or ghosts arriving in rooms by passing through walls. Everyone has solutions, with more

32

to say by not saying certain obvious things. Offers of visceral aid arrive, rides to counselors, complicated and embellished healthy food, books to levitate one's spirits, singing among others. Each day is worn on the body until the sensational night. Although night can start early. Problems wither and fly away. Neighbors might disagree or be disagreeable about empty bottles, bodies spilled onto a floor or yard, the smell of something like turpentine, vomit scattered and drying like old flowers.

To live on air. To give the body back like a betrayal. A silence permeates and spoken words snare.

* * *

I don't drink or attend parties much anymore. I have reassembled myself. I'm searching elsewhere for whatever form of happiness or acceptance I can find. I try new pursuits; learning Hebrew, tap dancing, art, grouting our house. I make numerous mistakes. Which I expect, the same way I bumble through life as I learn how to navigate my existence. Some errors are simply more prominent than others. On the nearby beach where I live now, in Seattle, I speak to sea lions, gulls, and crows.

Sometimes suddenly, a stranger is close and answering me. Or I misconstrue someone's reply to mean something. How many of my awkward gestures and wrong words could be interpreted as cruel, arrogant, or thoughtless? Communicating is a whole marriage. The best part about failure is that you can't do any worse. You're already at the bottom. But then it's time to do better, to recall what was done, deal with the pain, and compensate for shortcomings.

I have been laughed at for believing ludicrous statements people uttered to me. That an Italian diplomat spawned my sister. Or once, I was offered some chocolate treats that turned out to be dog treats. Or that crickets arrived from spaceships. I can be that naïve.

* * *

I dreamt my favorite party was where guests arrived as my

best dream or worst nightmare. Many people came dressed as themselves. The gathering was composed of my friends and family. My mother was a vampire, lacquering her face whitely, her lips blood red, and her body squeezing itself out of her clothes. My father, in a porkpie hat, hummed big band tunes, and smoked one cigarette after another until he turned into a pile of ash. My beautiful sister was glowing, growing wings and then she flew around, refilling everyone's drinks. One friend was a hurricane, another a computer, and another a giant cockroach. It was a red room stuffed with fluffy white pillows where trays of smoked eggs and salty poet's fingers were passed around.

* * *

So what is writing for? What is drinking for? To make ourselves feel better? How is that working? Some days I evaporate. I become a puddle that children jump over and tiptoeing adults avoid, afraid that they might drown in it. My mind fills up every time. It's about how to let those pesky ideas loose and do whatever flagrant thing they want. But the right tools could help, if only I knew what they are.

Every few years I want to throw a party, for a birthday, book launch, anniversary, whatever. Here, in Seattle, there are water views and people don't often dress up. I squint and try to look nice enough. My husband can go either way, no party or yes party, although he likes music and good food. Originally birthday celebrations began at the time of the ancient Egyptians, around 2345-2185 BCE, when the pharaohs were crowned and birthed as new gods.

I like mingling at other people's enormous weddings where there is an abundance of food and presents. I enjoy losing myself among happy people. I also like my anonymity. I can do anything. What exasperates me is the uninvited who can usurp a room since I'm becoming more curmudgeonly. Parties can be small or large, filled with friends, strangers, or simply strange friends, a family affair or a manner of expression. We certainly don't have enough fun in our lives. If a few people loiter for long enough, can I describe that as a party?

* * *

A party: music, balloons, appetizers, banners, horn blowers, candles, pinatas, confetti, wands, fake badges, masks, costumes, fake noses, beards or mustaches, wigs, silly cone hats, fog, crepe paper, cakes and cake toppers, flying numbers, stars, aliens, planets, rockets, drinks, drugs. Conversation. And presents, lots of presents.

* * *

I was wilder but now I'm tame. At a gathering quite a while ago, a red body suit I was wearing beneath my clothes unsnapped itself and rumpled out and over the back of my pants. A woman discreetly took me aside and asked, "What's that thing hanging over your butt?" That was one of the easier things to tuck back inside, but I wondered how long I had mingled with my underthing flapping about and no one mentioning anything.

I party now with starlings more than other people. I watch a field fill and empty of birds like a small celebration. Every landscape changes constantly and feels as if I'm beginning again. As clouds pass, the city appears through bare trees, with its buildings, cars, and people already stirring. I'm a part of something larger. I am sorry for being suddenly bird-less and thankful for being in the field. I gain more than I lose and can more easily surge towards something new, becoming more than what I say or do.

* * *

Shame is sometimes the outcome of mistakes and transgressions. Gin soothed and spoke to me in a way I wanted to hear. It explained some of the books I didn't understand, embellished my heart for my first husband, discussed the small-mindedness of the world, flicked away grief, and whisked me away from myself at the same time I felt closer to being myself. My bones hollowed while now they are heavier to drag around. I tried to remember each time I was drunk, but eventually I remembered less. I wanted gin to help me understand, but I couldn't trust it since I did things I couldn't recall. Sometimes I would drink more to feel better about whatever unsavory thing I'd just done.

* * *

At 94 years old, my mother still enjoys attending art openings, lobster nights at specific restaurants, celebrations, occasions, auctions, soirees, dinner parties, holiday festivities, balls, fashion shows, galas, awards, business launches, special events or performances. She lives in New York City and the fancier the event the better. She still likes being among people although she can't drink much anymore.

When I was young I watched my mother in various stages of undress, flirting between and during husbands, plunged into the midst of her abruptly changing moods, and I once heard her loudly having sex with a boyfriend.

It's appealing to leave parts of my life behind, burning down a house to heat a new home. A fresh me, me, me. But, hopefully, we do learn. Certain upheavals leave the body or the mind behind while engaging one's heart. I'm embezzling new cells, giving them names, inviting them to dinner, combining and recombining, asking their perspective on sleep and dreams and trying out pranks. In life it's good to look ahead.

In the future if I lean in as if to greet you at a gathering, I'll probably be listening.

II:

My Chosen Life

Everything that was here before me stays.
All the people I've known that have died sutured, into one person.
A grey hat that everyone else sees as a storm.
Me traveling in someone else's exotic landscape.
Someone rowing across an ocean to tell me something almost important.
Time held loosely inside.
All my questions answered out of order.
A house inside out like a dream, in a warm country.

36

Air no longer arguing with itself.
My human and nonhuman friends diagnosed correctly.
Complicated and beautiful sentences that forget to end.
All my dead cats meet each other in one room.
Completing the puzzle of my metaphorical heart.
Everything cracked open like an egg.

Questionable Party Themes:

> Performing miracles to unbelievers.
> Swapping complaints, discontents, or misgivings.
> Rubbing sticks, or something like them, together to start fires
> in small spaces.
> Commiserating with everyone who has just lost a job.
> Whispering to everyone who found this address in a toilet stall.
> Stroking people who have written excellent poems.
> Pinching convicts willing to discuss their crimes.
> Commending people with two or fewer diseases.
> Smiling at men who accidentally electrocuted someone while
> doing repairs.
> Listening attentively to people who resemble professors but
> aren't professors.

The Person Who Looks Like Me:

Pays people to help her but they leave her when they are done.
Practices apologizing to birds that would rather fly towards
clouds.
Has no philosophical understanding.
Starts to dig a hole to a place she hates.
Thinks night needs to be redecorated.
Calls you too often.
Just wants you for tonight.
Could have been made from apples.
Is going inside herself but wants to know what is in there first.
Prefers the company of animals.
Is playing a guitar in the subway and asking for money.
Believes everything you tell her.

- Laurie Blauner

WHAT IS THE MOON REALLY?

The moon is the anvil your grandfather
couldn't take with him into the grave.
The moon is the salt lick a lonely man
leaves in the yard so the deer will come
to his window while he sleeps.
The moon doesn't know where it's going,
though it goes there every morning.
The moon is losing its memory.
How long can it be allowed to live
by itself in that cluttered attic?
The moon is a young woman.
The moon is an old man who took
a shift no one else wanted long
ago and no one will switch.
The moon would like to just sit
on a beach somewhere and drink beer,
but it knows it would keep pulling the sea
towards it like a boy pulling the sheets up to his chin.
Then how would it read the Advanced Reader Copy
of the new novel sent by Goodreads?
The moon keeps its hands behind its back,
a boy told to be careful in the museum
so it doesn't knock into any stars.
The moon wants to know
can it count on your vote in the race
between the moon and the sun?
The moon says we have to live
within the two-party system
while dreaming of the trinity.
The moon has made its peace
with being loved by none
but drunks and poets.
The moon is content with renting.
The moon is a longshoreman,
a card-carrying member.

The moon is this page, it wishes
I'd just left it blank.
The moon is a mirror.
We see ourselves in it.
The moon wants to know
when are we coming back?
It liked the little kisses the astronauts
skipped into its face.
The moon is the girl who wants you
to come home with her,
to whom you say, "I shouldn't."
Go.
The moon wants to fall into your hands
like a silver apple you've been waiting for
to fall, standing night and day
under the tree so that
people are becoming concerned.
The moon is the son tasked with giving
the eulogy – in return he is given
plenty of space.
The moon is a child's rowboat drowned
under hailstones and willow leaves.
The moon stays awake so we can sleep.
But some nights the moon isn't there
when we look, like a guard who goes
missing the night of the assassination.
The moon is envious of the living
but knows how it always ends.
The dead love the moon most.
The moon makes them feel seen.
There are some who, dying,
ask for the bed to be wheeled over
to the window so they can die
in the moonlight.
The moon knows of these,
far away as she is.
She throws her light on them
like children throwing flowers

in a dog's grave.
The moon is the man chosen
for a lineup, who looks nothing
like who did it, but gets picked
by the witness and put on trial.
The moon is on trial for stealing
the sun's light, though the sun has plenty.
The sun is a corporation,
the moon a citizen like you and me.

- *Austin Smith*

Local Cyclist Struck In Bike Lane

I read the headline again, then a third time. Unfurl it down to the name, right below the occupation, and above the location: tristate.

I roll up the newspaper again. Think about gluing it shut so I can use it for a fly beater, but then I'd be living forever with those words somewhere in my house. *Neurosurgery… broken bone in his back… restore the use of his dominant hand…*

Push off from the dining room table. Pace a little. I should feel bad, yeah? After all, the girl who shared the fundraiser ($60,000! to get him on his feet again!) is a friend of mine.

I leave the paper in the living room. I take a trip to the market but leave my bike at home. Beneath florescent lights I test the weight of avocados against each other, assigning them gold, silver, bronze. Eventually, when I can't waste any more time, I go home, my basket still empty, the paper still on the table. I choose coffee. I would've chosen liquor if I'd had any.

Strange to think of him with a tube down his throat in an ICU somewhere. Strange to think of me, here, sipping my coffee when I know how he takes his: double shot of espresso, filled with hot water, a splash of milk. Two dollars in the tip jar. I give in. Rubber-necking, that's what this is. Pervasive interest. There's a photo of him and his brother here. I didn't know he had a brother. He didn't tell me that. He didn't tell me much of anything.

I'm imagining him with the tube down his throat but mostly remembering his face when I told him I was nineteen (the article says he's been riding professionally for almost 20 years), and the loofah in his bathroom it took too long to bring myself to ask about. Maybe that was cowardly - ignoring it, returning to his side, staring at the drink growing wet with condensation on his coffee table, the heat of his body next to mine.

I picture the way it had grown cold the day his wife

came home from work to find the two of us in the hot tub, clinking glasses, living it up like kings, her face contorting in rage and agony like something out of a movie (Alien, 1979). Think of how he hated her, until she was standing in front of him, and he was on his knees begging for forgiveness. When I close my eyes, I am back in his shower, porcelain pressed to my knees, hiding behind the curtain like it's shrubbery, listening to her scream through the walls about the bits of me I've shed around the house (a clip, stray blonde hair, a sweater).

My phone against my thigh goes off, but I ignore it, the shape of those texted words already burning in my memory, *how could you do something so stupid…*

I look back at the newspaper. They don't say much about the man who hit him, just that he was driving a sedan (four-wheel-drive) and had the right of way. There's a picture of the bike beside a bush on the side of the road, mangled and chewed up, folded like it's trying to hide and wishing for all of it to come to an end. Black words splashed up the page: *he may never ride again!* Tragedy, sure, or maybe penance, or maybe just retribution.

Can you truly pity a man who loses the use of his dominant hand when he's done so much ugly with it?

I don't know. I guess so.

*- **Tessa Swackhammer***

DISFIGURED DREAMING

though i was walking as fast as i could, the hospital hallway seemed endless. my best friend had just become a father. while running, i sensed i was dreaming and i knew i'd see my oldest friend for the first time. i also understood once i'd wake up, i'd never see him again: this friend did not exist in physical reality. when i had finally reached him, his face looked joyous and proud, holding his newborn baby up in the air. when he passed the infant to me, it gradually became clear that its head and face were horrifically deformed. observing its massively disfigured face and skull, i expected to wake up. to my shock, the baby gently snuggled against my chest. with a never felt before sense of exhilaration, warmth and love, i looked my oldest friend in the eyes and said, this baby is absolutely gorgeous. i could feel it in my bones that i truly meant it. perhaps that's why for the days afterwards, i was haunted by the thought that it should have been him to dream this dream and not me.

- Giorgia Pavlidou

AN EXISTENTIAL MISTAKE?

what was foreign
felt familiar
what was my own
felt unfamiliar

i left the foreign
& lost the familiar
to live among my own
as a foreigner

- Giorgia Pavlidou

THE ALCHEMY OF MISPERCEPTION

Ἐν ἀρχῇ ἦν ὁ λόγος, καὶ ὁ λόγος ἦν πρὸς τὸν θεόν, καὶ
θεὸς ἦν ὁ λόγος.

it's to a symphony of   symptoms   (that)
the silicone angels of misperception swing

    not out of malice   nor deceit   but implored by desire
    to embellish the unadorned word   painted by fear

i've seen these celestial drag queens undulate
moshing queerly as if hyper-feminine druids
                     priestesses of kitsch

    they orbit a curious choreography of freudian slips

    & as if they'd speak in tongues
their anatomies became consonants   their spirits diphtongs
      their shenanigans vowels

*are you listening to yourself? i can't hear you. what did you just
say? i didn't say anything. you must have heard something i
imagined. i think you asked a question; to which i said:*

in principio erat verbum et verbum erat apud deum et deus erat verbum

* * *

forgetting is an art   i think you said (did i?)
as dissimilar as two unasked questions
as incompatible as carbon and φλογιστόν
as merciless as compassion

& satan concurs : the word indeed is god but i've always been
prone to mishearing   spiritual atheism

i've been told they'll say they said (did they?) exactly what you
told me   which is a warehouse of borrowed statements

borrowed decibels equals   other peoples' words which are
also your words & my words

                    & these are the magnificent factories of words

word-machines
                    round as triangles pulled around the neck
prone to supernatural mishearing:

*the word is a living spirit being   all verdant greening   the
word is all creativity yet shrewd*

they mistook you for a living being   an angel of anarchy
an inverted *antiphon*
                    a name chanted in an underwater mass
                    sung by machines prone to mishearing
(one elongated mistake equals one prayer)

they misunderstood the tibetan book of the dead as prolonged
mishearing

   beauty is always bizarre i've been told & i do tend to agree

it's the word more than beauty (however beautiful) that ter-
rifies me
      more than what's inside a handful of dust

      the logos misspoken   misheard   misperceived
      impossible to unhear
      impossible to unsay (that)

      the sun's rays have calcinated   by mistake!

                                        - Giorgia Pavlidou

We Trashed Our Oceans

Rain was bucketing down as we drew into the mucky yard to pick up Bernard-Henri. A few beasts had been thrown some fresh straw in a corner and were chewing away, oblivious to the rain. Lucille's face was a rictus of disgust. Even though Bernard-Henri is her son and not mine, it was I who got out, picking my way carefully around rain-filled holes in my last pair of town shoes.

Before I got to the house door the farmer appeared. Mr. Léveillé was a man whose toothless chats I savored on deserted country roads when there was no one around. He would draw to a halt in an aged vehicle, a calf or a bale of hay in the back, and fill me in on the family I'd got involved with, or the village and its characters. The first few times he stopped he would check who I was. I now think he was pulling my leg.

Today he was brisk. "It's yourself." He waved at Lucille in the car. "Bernard-Henri got fed up waiting, he's gone on ahead, decided he'd collect the family from home first. It's not a great day for him to be missing from the farm, with the show over in R-. I have to go over there myself now. And it pissing down."

This explained the beasts in the yard. "I can see how a chair by the fireside would be preferable," I said.

"Civil servants," he shook his head and returned to the house. I got into the car and explained the situation.

"That's Bernard-Henri," said Lucille. "Just like his father – never there when you want them. Go straight to the nursing-home so."

"He was probably afraid Léveillé would give him a job to do while he waited," I said.

Lucille just ignored me.

* * *

When we got to the nursing home Bernard-Henri, wife, and children were piling out of their old van. The wife tended to put on a good show and still had some designer clothes from their

48

Paris days. Bernard-Henri was wearing a tracksuit in loud colors and logos, like someone heading to the gym. I supposed it was a welcome change from a cowman's outfit caked in mud or worse. His big head of rasta ringlets, considered monstrous by his mother and his grandmother, Giselle, was tied in a bundle at the back of his neck and tucked into an elongated snood in yellow and red wool.

"Are they African colors," Lucille hissed.

"Africa's not a country. They're the colors of the Norman flag too."

Lucille raised one eyebrow at me before heading over to kiss Bernard-Henri frostily then pecking rapidly at the cheeks of his wife and kids. As we headed indoors, Bernard-Henri muttered to me, "You'd wonder why the kissing, such as it is, has to be done in the rain."

Giselle, Lucille's mother, sat in her wheelchair in the middle of the retirement home dining area. A banner high above her head read: 'Giselle Le Tynevez: 100th birthday.' Photographers and journalists from the local papers crowded around her, and her four generations of descendants. There was laughter and talk about her going for a second century. The rest of the retirement-home residents watched from their usual dining tables around the room. Champagne abounded. Greetings cards wished Giselle a century of luck and happiness!

"What am I going to do with all these flowers?" she said, laughing.

Abundance had never been part of Giselle's life. When I first used to drop over to her place for a drink, I saw her darn synthetic pullovers anyone else would throw out, and noticed darns in cloth handkerchiefs and the knees of pantyhose. In those early days I was usually enlisting Giselle's support in pressing my suit with Lucille. Later it tended to be because mother and daughter were fighting and would only communicate through a third party, me.

Giselle's life had been anything but luck and happiness. She was convinced that her mother had died in agony because of Giselle's 'bad' marriage to a good-looking hard-worker called Bernard, who had an eye for the ladies. "Took up with sweetie-pies when I was in hospital having the babies," Giselle told me, "and later when I was in there having my equipment out." Her jewellery disappeared on that last occasion. "Gave it to a sweetie-pie, or one of them stole it."

But she loved Bernard, for he was what she called 'an original'. This was what had attracted her to him. He was proud and careful of his person, something she admired: "When he wanted to sleep on a train he'd tie a scarf under his chin and knot it to the rack above his head. He said he didn't want to look like an ape with his mouth open when he slept."

Today Bernard is gone (nursed patiently till the end) and Giselle looks happy and content. Her 100th birthday is happening at last, after months of worry over how it might go. "The best thing I can do when it's over is get on with it and die," she often said, obsessing about invitations and cost. Yet Giselle has always known how to rise to special occasions: I'd seen her whip gourmet dinners from precious little on the old stove in her kitchen, dealing with all comers according to her own calm rhythm.

A little menu stands at each place, with a photo of a laughing Giselle in a wide blue sunhat. The local journalist is genuinely laughing as she takes notes. Finally Giselle is wheeled into her central spot at the top table, and we are urged to sit. As a 'spare part' (living with, but not married to, Lucille) I am relegated to a seat opposite Bernard-Henri.

"My belly thinks my throat is cut," he says.

Smiling staff from the retirement home come around with warm hors d'oeuvres and cool white wine. Bernard-Henri – of an age to be my son too – seems restless, nervous, distressed even, and although he eats and drinks, he pays no heed to it. Liquids, solids, bread baskets, all arrive and accumulate around him: he neither serves himself nor passes them on.

The soufflé arrives, and more wine.

"Things are going down the toilet," Bernard-Henri says, gazing into his plate. "I see no way out of it. They'll squeeze us all until we explode. World War II was caused by everyone putting the financial squeeze on Germany."

I look around. No one is paying attention to us: Lucille is deep in political conversation with a local dignitary, and I wonder if he is one of those she frequented before she left her second husband. Bernard-Henri's wife, a child on her knee, is deep in women's talk with another woman. Bernard-Henri's adolescents are far away at the end of the dining area with the rest of the kids, comparing hardware and music.

"It's the immigrants that are costing us," he says.

The main course hasn't even appeared. I imagine Giselle doing her best to raise this sulky boy after Lucille abandoned husband and child and fled Giselle's agricultural universe of birth and death with its notions of good and bad reinforced by a still-powerful priest, all of which were hardly suitable for raising a child in our new world. Older, wearier by then, with other grandchildren often dumped on her, she'd have had little time to find out about all the new dangers lying in wait for people not toiling 24/7 to stay alive, as she and those before her had done. By then, farming as they'd known it was finished, and they were raising kids for Paris factories. Which is how my own parents ended up going all the way from Rouen to Paris. And this explains how the Norman idyll was transmitted from them to me, with its memories of summer holidays among a gang of cousins. Which is why I eventually requested transfer back to this provincial town. Parisian colleagues were mystified: "What're you going to do with yourself out there?" and "How will you amuse yourself?" they asked at my transfer party. The most sinister comment was, "Do you realize just how backward they are out there?"

Bernard-Henri has moved on to another subject, the suburb of Paris where he lived until recently. He says local taxes doubled there because the proportion of immigrants in high-rises is greater than that of respectable locals in small villas. "They're all on hand-outs," he says.

"That's not true," I venture. I've seen this as part of my job. "Illegal immigrants can't just come to France, have babies and collect hand-outs. People wouldn't live so far from their country and family just for that. And government isn't that soft. Immigrants are sacrificed. They have no choice but to get on with it and send the money home. It's all decided without them. They work days and nights and only sometimes sleep – in bunk beds in crowded rooms in insanitary buildings."

Bernard-Henri smiles slyly. I have made the fatal mistake of engaging discussion.

"The ones I used to supervise didn't want to work," he says darkly. "They hid in the toilets in case they'd be asked to do anything."

* * *

We finish the main course and start on the cheese.

"Who's going to sing a song?" asks Giselle.

At big dinners in our corner of Normandy everyone is expected to do a turn – tell a joke, sing, get a rise out of someone else. The rest of France has forgotten.

One or two people oblige, with old favorites like 'Under the Bridges of Paris' and another about Marguerite who makes 'good frites,' an obvious metaphor for her sexual prowess.

One by one, Giselle's friends and acquaintances from all over the home are wheeled into an empty space beside us. They share a glass with her. In drinking terms, Giselle can still hold her own with the best of them.

The table is too wide. The first visitor, wheeled into place by his wife – also a resident – shouts and fails to make Giselle hear him. He gives up and turns to me.

"I was deported, you know – five years' work-camp in Czechoslovakia."

Bernard-Henri drops whatever he is grappling with. "What kind of work?"

"Agricultural."

Bernard-Henri loses interest immediately.

"What did you do when you finally got back here?" I ask.

"Agricultural work." The old man shrugs at my stupid question. "The Charlotte is the queen of potatoes."

Bernard-Henri shows signs of impatience.

I turn my full attention to the old gentleman in the wheelchair. He is small and thin and stares ahead of him as he speaks.

52

"But I lost the desire to sing," he says. "And I felt even less like singing when I came back." He turns towards me. "The wife could never understand it."

Bernard-Henri watches a member of staff come to check on Giselle, giving her a kiss on the cheek. I notice she is the only one to actually touch Giselle. A family thrifty with love.

"Waitress!" Bernard-Henri calls out to the girl. "Could we get some more wine over here?"

"She's a member of staff, not a waitress," the old gentleman says, turning towards Bernard-Henri.

"So?" says Bernard-Henri.

With the corner of my eye I see him shovel cheese into his mouth from a knife.

"You promised you'd sing," Giselle shouts at me. "You said we'd sing."

So I do, from a book that members of staff pass round. As I sing into a microphone I am surprised to notice Giselle still searching for the singer. I sing and wave but she doesn't get it.

When I finish and before I can engage the old man in conversation again, he whispers urgently, as if asking for help, "I'm losing the run of myself."

Abruptly, his wife knocks the brake off his chair and wheels him away.

I am stuck with Bernard-Henri again. I wonder when Lucille will rescue me. Bernard-Henri and I have nothing in common except Lucille. I came across her in my administrative capacity after my arrival from Paris in the early days of my Norman idyll. It was the land of plenty with lush vegetation climbing over walls and hedges – you planted something, and it grew. Beasts thrived. People were tough and thrifty. I loved the cob houses, so ecological they were back in fashion again. I found Lucille, who'd wanted out of it all, had managed to flee but had been so unhappy she'd come back again. From her I learned there was no idyll: in the country you fit in or leave. If they don't like you, they throw weed killer on your garden, slash your tires, engage in administrative skullduggery. Phone calls come in to my office to tattle with information, true or not, that's designed to send the authorities crawling all over the enemy. It keeps them all busy and at each other's throats. Lucille, knowing who's who, picks her way through it all. I walk alongside, knowing nothing. Giselle occasionally marks my cards. She can do nothing to save me from Lucille.

Bernard-Henri has moved on to android phones. He seems to know the price of everything, including the 3,000 Euro it costs to have one's eyes lasered for short-sightedness.

"You're hardly the age to be short-sighted," I say.

His eyes glaze over, and he begins to talk of his time in Paris.

"There was a time when 3,000 Euros was nothing to me," he says. "I'd go to a restaurant at midnight and call for oysters and champagne. Money was no object. You got into debt and got out of it as quickly. That's impossible now."

He sighs. "It was because of all that that we left Paris for a new, cleaner life here. No going back. I'd even like to think I'm carrying on a family tradition. My grandfather was a cowman, too." He eyes me carefully. "Did you know that?"

"I haven't heard everything yet," I say.

"You certainly haven't. You're a bit of a mystery yourself." He laughs, and then he tells me about Giselle's first husband, the one before Bernard.

"Killed in the war." I nod.

"Not exactly." He's still smiling. "He was burying a German corpse. Said it wasn't Christian to leave it lying on the road, even though it might be booby-trapped."

"And?"

"He and two others dragged it into a field, dug a hole and put the body in. 'Before we cover it,' Giselle's first husband – the one she loved – said, 'Let me do one last thing. This is for what you've done to us,' and he whacked the body with the back of the shovel. It was booby-trapped. Exploded in his face."

The afternoon is growing tired of us. Bernard-Henri's wife looks into space. We have finished dessert and await release. Lucille has moved on to chat with the man who runs the

54

home. I have heard rumors that she slept with him to speed up the process of getting a room for Giselle. Greater love than this.

My final chance for release appears when another character is wheeled into position on my left. This one comes armed with his own fat songbook. He appears to be Giselle's special friend, probably because he sings. It is a noteworthy coincidence that he bears the same name as Giselle's good-looking husband. For Bernard-Henri's name they strung his two grandfathers' names together. Now everyone jokes about him having the same name as a famous French philosopher. "Famous French wanker," our Bernard-Henri says, "white shirt open to his waist. He's got it up here, though," he adds, pointing at his temple.

This other, older Bernard sings romantic songs of past love and love unrequited. Each time he stops, Giselle looks over at me and shouts, "You promised we'd sing."

It dawns on me that she can't work out who is singing, because the sound is coming from the speakers behind her and seems to bear no relation to the people holding the microphone. She is too far away for me to explain. This is torture. Torture for Giselle, her friends, her family, me. Even Bernard-Henri is in a worse state than all the physically crocked around us who made it through two wars.

I can't help any of them. Later Lucille will say the whole thing has exhausted her. She'll want to drink more. Eventually she'll have a migraine. She will say that Bernard-Henri probably votes far-right. She will not relate her conversations with various men all afternoon.

At last Giselle's great-grandkids get hold of the microphone and start singing their own songs, songs they know by heart and sing earnestly. Three skinny and one plump girl, their backs to us, concentrate on phonefuls of music, their backs jigging to the rhythm. Giselle looks around for a singing child and at last a great-grandchild throws her arms around her, and they sing together into the microphone from one of the old books.

"My youngest," Bernard-Henri says. "She wants to go

into show-business." He doesn't look happy about this either. "The others never sing at all. Headphones dangling, they just listen to stuff the rest of us can't hear – and wouldn't want to."

"The singing gene skipped two generations!" Giselle shouts across at us above the singing, happy, finally.

Bernard-Henri whips out his phone. "I have my own blog, you know."

I'm impressed.

"I use it to talk about the state of the world," he says. "Did you know that there are albatrosses in Hawaii which die from hunger with their stomachs full of plastic?"

He scrolls his screen helpfully to a list of items found in the birds' stomachs:
- •Plastic children's toys
- •Colored balls
- •Buttons
- •Bottle tops
- •Bits of nylon fishing nets
- •Cigarette lighters
- •Tampon applicators

"We trashed our oceans." He swipes the screen again. "Ready for the photos?"

And there they are, photo after photo of dead albatrosses. Each carcass is a two-dimensional bird in flattened dirty feathers, with a collection of colored plastic items where their stomachs were: surprisingly big and round – and chock-full of objects.

"The birds haven't been moved or the photos re-touched," Bernard-Henri lectures me.

Lucille catches my eye from the other end of the table: she has finished hustling and is ready to go. She throws daggers' looks at Bernard-Henri and will not approach while he is in conversation with me. I must make a move.

He pauses over details: there are lots of bottle tops. Some of the birds seem to have gone for one color: some stomachs contain mostly blue items, others mostly red. I wonder where Bernard-Henri found the photos, but I'm not going to ask.

56

"I left the city to save the planet," he says, smiling. "The idea! It can't be saved by me, or the likes of old Léveillé."

"There's worse than him," I say.

"I suppose he's better than our philosophic wanker," he says. He rises and signals to his wife, "I'm outside for a rollie." He disappears.

Meanwhile, Giselle's other children sit tightly, not touching her or each other. Another daughter produces a dog-eared document about Giselle's parents a century ago. The talk moves to WWI and the time their father was transferred to a big city to fill shells, stripped to the waist, pouring with sweat. After a month, he wrote to say he couldn't stand it without them, and demanded that his family come live with him. So their mother left Brittany lumbered with all of them plus baggage for an indefinite period. Giselle recounts the trip, the memory still vivid and violent: their loving mother panicking as the train began to move, hurling the youngest sisters onto the floor of the carriage and the bags after them. Forgetting the picnic basket behind them on the platform. Even now Giselle looks shocked. There followed a day's wait in some station with no food or money. Soldiers fed them bread and sardines. In the city, their first house was a basement. You had to climb up a ladder to look out the window until the father moved them to a place where they could see the outside world.

There is silence after this story, its separate and discrete details obviously true, colored by a memory that has forgotten or never knew their context and completeness, from a mind that is a century old.

A voice at the back of the room begins to roar. "I want to go home!" The huge angry voice of a lone man at a solitary table bounces around the big room and off the heads of Giselle's party. "Home! Outa here!"

There is silence for a number of seconds. Giselle's family smile and pretend this isn't happening. Sounds of the same songs from another reception next door almost sound like rivalry.

Lucille gets up quickly and unbrakes her mother's wheelchair.

Giselle, clutching her songbook, commands the fourth generation: "Bring those flowers to my room."

People swing into action. Distant relatives get lost in corridors.

On arrival in the room, Giselle's roommate, her trembling hand as usual in mid-air as if she might say something – if there were time, if anyone would listen – is cut off from her late afternoon soap by a parade of people bearing flowers and looking for surfaces for them.

Kids look up at adult faces and try to scrute their intentions.

Giselle's 100th is all over, and she can die in peace.

* * *

A week later we brought Giselle the photos. She scrutinized the faces of her children, their children, their children's children, and decided which photos might be kept, installed in albums, framed.

"We sang a few good songs, in the end," she said. She pointed to a photo with Bernard-Henri: "He could have worn something more appropriate. But then he was badly brought up."

Lucille didn't rise to the bait. I assumed that if I weren't there they'd have had a slanging match.

On the way home in the car Lucille was silent. I said, "It's over and done, and it all went very well."

She stared straight ahead.

I wanted to say how I would miss Giselle when she went, as I already missed her ever-open door, her well-stocked drinks cupboard, her groaning table. I would miss her stalwart endurance, her propensity to laugh and talk about things close to her heart. Giselle's generation had expressed affection through feeding and cleaning and mending and the occasional slap on the butt. They were optimistic; they sang their own songs. I wanted to talk about an island of plastic six times bigger than France that was floating in the Pacific. I wanted to ask if we, the Peace and Love generation – in spite of our easier life – had allowed the planet to decline and love to become a

58

spare part. Content to listen to others sing, we expressed love via technology and purchases. I also knew we were more to be pitied than blamed – all of us. I wondered if hardship produced endurance and if hardship was what we lacked most.

Of course I couldn't say any of that, because Lucille was still running hard. She originally fled Giselle's world because she couldn't stand it – and it didn't like her much either. When she found that elsewhere was worse, she ran back to Normandy again, only to be treated like a fly on the soup, with no real role or place. All this made her run around and drink. It made me love her. Somehow she and I had to pick the bones out of it.

I thought I saw her shiver. At the crossroads I slowed, and she said curtly, "Pull in at the *Tout Va Bien*. I feel the need of a cognac or three."

- Mary Byrne

Silvia wakes up to her name in the paper. Third page, nothing major, just a black and white photo of a small, crude cross with her name on it. Instead of dates, a number she does not recognize: 11. She scrambles to get ready for work, picks up a crumpled shirt from the floor. She'll save that for later: it happens, hers is a common name after all. Silvia B., pre-school teacher, single. During the drive to school, her phone keeps ringing but the Roman traffic is too distracting to even consider picking up. Then the mad rush to find a parking spot, gushes of February wind pushing her all the way to the school.

Kids crying, then laughing. Lunch time and a glance at her phone, so many missed calls. She tries her sister, gets no answer — no surprise, she must be at work too. Why did she call on a Tuesday morning, though? The parents' calls start coming late in the day. A father comes in and signs off his kid in a hurry, without stopping for a greeting or even waving goodbye, the little girl wide-eyed, too surprised and rushed to even enjoy the unexpected treat of escaping in Daddy's arms. The main office phone keeps ringing all afternoon. Silvia reads the naptime story, her voice a little uneven. There is a strange tremor in her pulses, a sense of danger impending like a cruel word only partially heard, a face half-remembered in a dream. Something lurking at the edge of her consciousness, impossible to capture though solidly there, taking form and weighing her down. When she's called to the office, she's not surprised.

"You killed your baby," the voice says just before Ms. A. opens her mouth. "You killed her, and now they know." "Unwed, sinful," they say.

It didn't go like that, or not quite: the tone was bland, slightly worried. Bad publicity for the pre-school, an unfortunate case, truly displeasing. Of that conversation she now remembers very little, as she walks in the fading light. Her abortion is in the paper, in plain sight: her name the one visible in the picture, though many others are listed in the article. The babies needed burials, a private association paid for a large plot and picked the plain, white crosses. "There was no baby," she says to herself, and then, softly, "eleven weeks, no longer a heartbeat." Nearly one-hundred crosses crowd the plot like small dreams half forgotten. On each, the name of a woman, now forcefully, forever a mother: a cemetery for women only, women who still live. Silvia walks the streets in a daze. Just after sunset, she enters the park. She walks, she sits, the rush of blood in her ears deafening. Then she quiets down, she listens. What calls for her from the hollowed trunks of the trees? Does the day die into smooth darkness, inside? Can she enter the trees' soft obscurity and never come back, growing as one with their calm, patterned life? Silvia gets up, forgetting her phone on the bench. She crouches down by the tree closest to her. It keeps calling, softly. She listens to its slow song, remembers the pattern. Her feet grow roots, her limbs twist in unknown obscurities, her hair is starting to glow with the red tints of autumn. She rests and forgets, a new, vegetable life running smooth in her veins, unveiling mysterious re-births.

There's no longer a name on the cross, no longer a woman close to the branches. Silvia breathes with the trees, and sings quietly to herself. Eleven weeks. Not forever. There's peace in the hollows of trees.

- Federica Santini

A Toast to the End of the World

I meet M. at a work party when the host sits us across from each other. We are being served sharply balanced Martinis in vintage coupe glasses and bland appetizers on plastic trays. We don't speak beyond introductions, each engaged in separate, low-voiced conversations with the young men at our side, mine pale and faintly toxic, hers milder, wide grinned.

After dinner, she comes and stands next to me when I pause to look at the night garden outside. She raises a delicate hand, tucking her hair behind her ear to reveal a shaved strip beneath, the twisted design of a small snake sharp on her scalp. I stare, frozen in place, wanting to touch it, but she lets a glossy lock fall into place with a sideways glance. As she shifts her pose, our hands almost touch. Behind the French doors, the new leaves on the pear tree smirk at me, their silvery glint reflecting the glow of her downturned lids.

"I will see you out there," she says.

Before I can find something to say, my young man joins us, his firm hand on my shoulder guiding me back to the crowd and away from a longing unknown to me, a stirring of something just seen and then lost. My legs barely functioning, I steady myself against a chair, the small snake, tattooed on the inside of my eyelids, making me dizzy.

Through the evening, I seek out her eyes but M. seems to avoid me, enthralled in whispered remarks with her broad-shouldered friend. As most of the guests saunter down the long hall to retrieve their coats, my fiancé's tense smile lets me know it's time to go. He dislikes my still feeling unsteady, blames it on drinking and eating too little, displeasure sharp in his voice. I look up at the garden, see her standing outside by the pear tree. Drink in hand, she toasts in silence to the end of this night, raising her glass with eyes locked on mine. My ankle twists suddenly, one of my heels broken. I almost fall. By the time I look up again, she's inside, leaving, light on the arm of her young man. There's no one outside by the tree.

Next I hear, they have married. Then we have. My own

honeymoon begins when hers ends, her firstborn precedes mine by two months. At night I dream of her glowing lids, of my fingers pausing to follow the curved shape above her left ear. One day as I shave under the shower, my thighs perfectly smooth as he wants them, I bring the blade to my hair, below the tangled mass at the nape of my neck. I shave a small section, start cutting deeper. The blood wakes me up; I can see her face looking up from my bathroom mirror, calling for me. My kids call from the hall and she's gone.

I'm frozen in time, longing for her. Year after year, I receive sparse news: her sons growing up, entering school, graduating college. I still see her at night, farther away by the pear tree. Time stops and dilates, our husbands advancing in their careers, her elder son becoming a junior partner in a big firm. Her broad-shouldered young man aged, sick, then gone, as mine went just a few months before — over twenty years and still a stranger, an unwanted hand guiding me by the shoulder through a path I was never able to follow, steadying me up in anger when my heels fail me.

She visits more often, through mirrors and window panes, her reflection still thrilling at the core of my body, tingling deep in my flesh. I dream of us stepping out together that night, to sit under the pear tree, our hands locked. The silvery leaves form a curtain to hide us, keeping us safe. I drink from her glass, caress the snake by her ear and follow its shape down her pale neckline.

Now we are here, frozen in time. Drinks in hand, the years have washed out in the glitter of leaves. I press my lips to the coupe glass in my hand, then raise it in silence.

- Federica Santini

GUN! GUN! GUN!

I don't know about you, but for more than half
of my seven decades of life I've been cautious
around cops—not because I fear them, but because

I know they are fallible and can mistake
something I'm holding as a weapon.
I know this is relatively easy for me to say,

since I'm white, and I know bad cops have killed
good people who are not white for no good reason.
I also know there are cops, perhaps most cops, who

are more likely to shoot someone who is not white
than someone who is white, which is prejudice,
plain and simple, and is flat out wrong. What

I don't know is why anyone, particularly someone
who is not white, would hold something in the dark
that could be mistaken for a weapon, which is

just about anything one might hold if one is
not white, judging by what happens so frequently,
so a cop yells "Show me your hands! Gun! Gun!

Gun!" and twenty shots are fired in rapid succession
and a guy with a cellphone is shot dead, a guy
with only a cellphone, no gun, no knife, no weapon

at all, a guy who is not white, who personally
cannot argue the cops were prejudiced because
all he had was a cellphone and now he is dead.

And for saying this I may be vilified, because
it will seem I am blaming the victim, who, frankly,
may not be blameless, and forgiving the cops, who,

frankly, cannot be forgiven, because if they are
good cops, they will agonize for the rest of
their lives, and if they are bad cops, won't care.

- Matthew J Spireng

A Tree Called Delores

A burl is a tree growth in which the grain has grown in a deformed manner in response to an environmental injury.

When my husband Sam told me that my adoptive mother had died, I felt relief. It's not what you may think—that she had some terrible terminal illness, was in agony and death was a welcome release. She had created a wound in the central core of me, the burl invisible until she died.

We lived in a cabin without electricity and telephone, 48 miles outside of Whitehorse. I was sitting with our son Finn in our double wide chair, his little body leaning against mine, in front of our wood stove. As Sam walked towards us, his mouth opened and shut, making a snapping sound like the logs in the fire.

"Your sister called me at my office. She didn't want to tell you on the radio phone that Dolores died," he said.

I looked at the snapshot of Dolores that I had pinned to the wall. I am sitting on her lap, my face lost in the shadows, my fingers intertwined like the church without the steeple—I loved that finger game.

"Go back and wash them again," my mother would say, sending me back yet again to wash my hands.

Returning, I held them in front of her.

"See how white they are," she declared with a smile.

Maybe she thinks the brown will wash off, I thought to myself. It didn't. I always felt dirty.

Finn's gurgle split the silence. Perhaps Sam didn't know what to say after laying those words at my feet, like he had delivered a distasteful package or some sort of ultimatum. We weren't doing that well together. His pot smoking allowed him to be somewhere else most of the time, instead of where I needed him the most. The early arrival of our fragile son, who he didn't want, who he now loved, added logs to the wall that was growing between us. I was home for a few months on maternity leave and filled the quiet days trying to be normal.

* * *

66

For years now, I entertained thoughts about what I wanted from my parents' house. It was filled with antiques, some of which had been in my father, Daniel's, family for generations. I felt that if I had something from it, like their mahogany coffee table or their pine love seat, I'd be connected somehow and feel part of the family, like I had been born into it. My father's death a few months previously had left my mother's life on pause, like she was waiting for someone to tell her how to live.

* * *

As the morphine dripped its slow drip into my father's veins, I called my mother to tell her that I'd made plans to fly down to see him. He had burls too. Maybe they withered as he himself withered on his deathbed.

"Don't come. It will be harder on me if you come home!" Her words shot from our radio phone like splinters, to lodge in the deepest part of myself.

* * *

Daniel and Dolores adopted me when they were in their mid-forties. We moved often from small town to small town where my brownness stood out like coffee stains on a white carpet. Perhaps they hoped I would bridge their disenchantment with each other and life in general. They were of The Greatest Generation and had done their best to fit into post WW II society, but when I helped to shoulder their pain, their damage became my damage.

I had bought them a plaque for their 45th wedding anniversary and it hung above my father's calendar and his weekly lottery tickets. On August 21st, he had written the initials G.D.I.J.D.

When I asked him what the letters meant, he shared that on this day, my mother screamed, God Damn It Just Die. These letters etched their way into the box of grudges that he passed on to me after he died.

* * *

When my father was alive, my parents would have conversations through their dog Susie.

"What would you like for dinner, Susie?" my father would call out.

"Pork chops," my mother would yell from the den where she was sitting in her colorful muumuu, knitting yet another bootie, for the babies in the hospital.

She wasn't physically capable of volunteering anymore so she knitted. I followed in her footsteps to fill my free time with volunteering before I was old enough for paid work. I won the Volunteer of the Year award when I was fourteen, and was interviewed on our local TV station.

After Susie passed away, my mother didn't want to get another pet, declaring, "it's getting too hard to say goodbye." The thought of her sitting in a quiet house that echoed with the ghosts of pet arguments long past prompted me to buy her a stuffed long-haired dog that looked so real that you listened for its bark. 'Sammy' sat with her on the couch and as her knitting needles clacked, he watched what she watched, the TV mostly on mute—she hated commercials.

* * *

"You couldn't even come home when he was dying," my mother snapped, and I could feel the splinters start to fester. I knew they would poison me for years. Like my father, I'm a holder of grudges; their poison accumulates sap-like to slow my limbs and heart and eventually I'll be immobile. When my voice rose to respond, she hung up and our cabin stung with static. Now all our neighbors up and down the highway knew what a terrible person I am. Years later I wondered if she had even remembered telling me not to come home.

I'd love that rosewood stand, or, Geez, I wonder if those walnut chairs could fit, or, What about those ebony handled knives, I would muse to myself as I looked out the picture window at the crooked pine tree that I had nicknamed Dolores. It had a bird feeder resting on one of its lower limbs. She loved all animals—our house growing up had overflowed with them—and it reverberated with birds and squirrels and life.

The year that my father died, my mother and I had a disagreement. We had been talking about the politically correct way of addressing certain groups of people. When she remarked, "a true Canadian is White," our conversation ended like the slice of an axe. For the first time, I didn't go home for Christmas and with my father now gone, my mother spent it at my sisters' house.

I looked out our window at the pine, now frosted, and thought about what my sister had told me when she and my mother were at the hospital sitting vigil and the social worker had stopped in for a visit.

"Daniel, tell Dolores that you love her," she had urged my father.

He had turned his face away, silent. I visualized a slash appearing in their Anniversary plaque—the sap dripping across my father's calendar to pool on the floor. I felt compelled to tell my mother that I loved her and called her at my sisters' house to wish her a Merry Christmas.

"Love you too," my mother replied, her voice sounding small and far away. We agreed to talk again in a couple of weeks.

* * *

I stood with the radio receiver in my hand, asking the operator to please try again. Outside my window, the pine tree shivered in the still air, lonely without the canopy of squirrels and birds and eerie without the squawk of whiskey jacks.

"No answer," she responded, her voice flat. Was there a hint of reproach?

I found out later that the police had to break down her front door to find her dead on her bathroom floor, her gnarled body like an effigy amidst discarded cigarette butts.

* * *

In their bedroom, my parents had a wooden box that was carved by my grandfather—a carpenter like my father—and as a child, its energy called to me. I remember fingering a faded invitation to a dance and recalled an older relative confiding how my parents in their younger days loved to dress up to go out dancing. I picked up a wooden pendant engraved with two

D's inside of a heart that said, "I love you," rolled it between my fingers, tasted it with my tongue and put it under my pillow with plans to return it. I wanted to have something of her from when she was happy.

* * *

I looked at Sam still standing in front of me. He shifted his weight from one foot to another like a child who couldn't wait for recess as I fingered the engraved D in the pendant around my neck.

"We have to do better," I said. "You and I, we need to do better, right?"

We looked out the window at the pine tree that danced in the wind.

- Charmaine Arjoonlal

First Instinct

You swore you would destroy mankind—
your favorite creation—begin again,
perfectionist you are. Wash away
your brightest mistake—made too much
in your likeness—before it was too late.
And who could deny you had the right?

Whatever virtue you sensed in Noah
that gave you pause, the tenderness of heart
that tempered your rage, your stubborn plan
for man as gentle steward of your estate—
hindsight shows your first instinct was right.
This project was bound to get out of hand.

This creature, so quick to divvy
your bounty, opposing hands eager
to cut and build, mine and sell, harvest
and consume—you should have stopped us
before mathematics, Newton, Wall Street,
the atom bomb, combustion engine, DDT.

Earth might have remained a perfect
blue marble. Societies of ants and bees,
thriving industry of coral reefs,
life's great play without greed or hate.
It should have been clear to you from day one
how badly we would fuck this up.

- Alfred Fournier

It's True

the forests are burning, that better and better
gadgets won't save us. We can't undo
devastation we've wrought on every species.

The hole in the sky spins like a severed eye.
Those who've seen our world from orbit—
blue, blue, blue—
were not the first to understand. It's time

to unravel the gods we created to justify
dominance. The last plate has been placed
on the table. Our hearts, carved into bowls,

finally holding all the beauty we'd abandoned
sweet as a meadow on the lip of spring.
Each of us carrying our few perfect joys
like prayerbooks to the funeral for the world.

- Alfred Fournier

On Being Patient

I have been transferred from the psychiatric hospital to an outpatient facility a mile down the road. When I call this place my final abode, Alison objects. I defend this with what I term objective reality. This was also objected to by Alison, who calls me objectively obtuse, which I take as the opportunity to push her further. "So, you're telling me this isn't my final home," I say. "Don't tell me this isn't an improvement on my situation, because it is. Anything is. This is my sanctuary." To which Alison whispers, "Halfway house," then leaves me to finish my unpacking.

* * *

Sanctuary. In the dictionary this word refers to safety, of course, but derives from the Latin word sanctuarium; a safe place for someone or something being chased, or hunted—a place of safety. "Safety from what?" I thought. Not to be too hard on myself, but I think we all know the answer. Looking further down the page, I see the expression sanctum, which can be traced back to a sacred, uninterrupted space. When I share this research with Alison she says, "I see your thinking is somewhat useful to you, but it's a bit, you know, dull."

* * *

On moving in, it strikes me how rundown this place is. The woman at the front desk stifles a hello, and yawns as she does so. The yawn, with all its assumptions of me, died in her mouth. Dressed in an auxiliary nurse's uniform, she's a gargantuan blob of a woman; her collar low and loose around the neck, her face and body inflated to the point of my disgust. She tells me that despite the clear lack of funding, they take great pride in placing outpatients among the community.

* * *

My apartment here is sparse with minimal furniture, the lino floor a yellow tinge of grey. When I move the sofa away from the blare of the twins in the apartment next door, it leaves its

73

negative imprint in the lino. I check the bathroom mirror, brushing my hand over what hair I have left on my head. I'm careful to comb my hair down; this urge to pluck strands from my head has created a patch of early onset baldness.

* * *

When my mother died twenty-five years back, my father found himself struggling. With approval from the family doctor, I was quickly admitted to the local psychiatric hospital. From the outset, my psychologist referred to my challenge as paranoid schizophrenia—but in my opinion, the voice in my head is more of a kindred spirit than a hindrance.

* * *

Treatment. Lunatic asylums, jail, insulin coma, metrazol shock, electro-convulsive therapy and frontal-leukotomy are all now pushed to the back of the medical bookshelves. In later days the psychiatric nurse leaned towards antipsychotic agents to manage my care. Having failed to respond to lithium, I am now on a course of quetiapine to give my mind balance. It was supposed to silence the delusions, to pave the way towards halfway house freedom. Now that I've moved to the outpatient's facility, my psychiatrist tells me that I can still make something of myself; that to all intents and purposes, a high I.Q. can lead to academia, possibly teaching. Somehow this carrot seems ever so distant, given the many years of stick.

* * *

Late at night I hear the softness of Alison's voice. Sometimes just fragments of a sentence. Other times, her words seem clearer. Her sound; a flute, the light wisp of reed that trembles in her voice. Whenever Alison speaks to me in hushed tones, we are at one. She forewarns, she alerts, she lets me know when things are not right. Her inner beauty is everything—my heart dips whenever we're apart.

* * *

At this point, I wish to point out there had been long moments of quiet in my head. Moments where I felt lonely. Hours would pass where I was lost in the silence. I took walks outside. I wrote letters to her at the bench by the lake. And when her voice returned, my heart warmed, and we would lose ourselves in conversation. Dr. Keller, my psychologist, has made it her mission to eradicate Alison from my life.

* * *

It's dark outside and I'm lying in my bed. I leave the curtains open to the glow of the moon spreading out over the canopy of trees, their heavy branches hanging still. I hear a noise coming from my door.

"Did you hear that?"

"Shh," she says.

I listen. I'm about to get out of bed when there's a clunk.

"What was that?" I listen some more. Another noise - muffled this time. "They're watching me again."

"I don't hear anything," she says, "go back to sleep."

"A little reassurance from your side wouldn't go amiss you know."

"   Are you trying to annoy me?" she whispers.

"Sometimes," I say, "I think you ignore me on purpose."

"Don't be daft."

"Sometimes, "I say, "I think, that you think I'm one of the crazy ones."

"Shh baby," she says.

I walk over to the window and check through the curtains. Outside I see dark shadows reaching out across the rear lawn towards me - a sole black swan drifts across the lake with only his reflection for company. With his left leg tucked behind his wing, the light wind steers him freely through the darkness.

* * *

Sometimes I watch the other outpatients in this place looking lost and forlorn in their rooms, pendulums with no sense of time, rocking themselves back and forth on their beds. I feel for them, and when possible, I try to help where I can. Earlier, I met a guy trying to hang himself from the upstairs banister. I told him that without a knot inside the loop, he was setting himself up for nothing but failure, frustration, and heavy bruising.

* * *

The next morning after breakfast there's a knock at the door. Through the laminated security glass, I recognise her outline. The grey hair. The blue anorak. So predictable.

"She's got that coat on again hasn't she?" Alison asks.

"What?"

"I bet you're going to let her in, too, aren't you?"

"Shh." I reach for the door handle.

"Stupid woman acts as if she owns you," she says.

The psychiatrist forces a smile as I open the door. "Hello, Robert." She puts an inflection on the end of my name, like I'm an errant child.

"You'll be wanting tea," I say.

"Tea? Oh yes."

I turn towards the kitchen. "I'll put the kettle on."

"I trust you took your tablet this morning." She takes a seat with her coat across her lap.

"Stupid bitch," Alison says.

The psychiatrist rises from her chair and circles the room. Opening the curtains, she eyes the framed photo of my mother sitting on the windowsill.

I show her the canister. "I've stuck to my routine. Look, I've got them here, see?"

"Any signs of Alison recently?"

"Whore," Alison says.

"No, nothing—not a peep," I say.

"You look distracted. You must keep up your meds."

I nod. I see where this is going. I take a breath to slow my breathing.

"What happens when you fall behind on your meds?" she asks.

"Just tell her where to get off," Alison says.

"You're not helping," I say, tussling strands of hair between my thumbs and forefingers.

"On the contrary," the psychiatrist says, "this is me, helping you." She puffs up the lone cushion on my sofa.

"I'll tell you if I ever forget or fall behind," I say.

"And?" she says.

"If I fail to do that, I go back to the hospital."

She looks at me over the rim of her glasses. "And wouldn't that be awful for you, Robert?" She takes my hand. "Let's see you take it then."

My smile drops. Any resistance will send out the wrong signal. And going back will mean windowless wards, security systems, and forced quetiapine dosage.

* * *

Sunday. The noise begins after breakfast, and I step out of the bathroom to hear the Samuel twins in the apartment next door. They moved into this facility a month before me, and I have it on good authority that they see themselves as musical maestros, leading violinists within a concert orchestra. Yet I hear them grinding their bows across their violins night after night, their doors and windows wide open for all to hear. If you take a 1920s steam locomotive, jam on the brakes, and listen to it scream down the track, you'd pretty much be there. And just to be clear, they're not twins, they just share the same name. Everyone seems to go along with this just fine.

At times like this, when it all gets too much, I sense Alison's presence—I slow my breathing until my chest is almost still. Starting at my feet, I work my way up to my chest and locate where she is. I sense her in the pit of my stomach.

"Are we good?"

"You should have left her at the door," she says.

"I can't do that."

"She wants you to herself."

"I think she just wants what's best for her patients."

"Whose side are you on?"

"Listen, I…"

"Next time," she says, "you listen to me."

"Yes," I say.

"Do you understand?"

"Yes."

"This thing we have. It works both ways. Nothing's ever permanent."

I make my way to the bathroom and open the cabinet. Toothbrush. Toothpaste. Shaving cream. Bic safety razor. I change it for a fresh one and apply the cream to my face. I rinse my razor and return it to the shelf. Taking my bottle of quetiapine, I open the lid and pour the contents onto the sink. I feel Alison watching me as I count out the remaining six tablets, one after the other.

* * *

That evening I see the clouds covering the sky, and a gentle breeze flicks my curtains back and forth. I feel Alison is close—I picture her face, the texture of her skin, the essence of her smell. I imagine the contours of her body against mine as our legs curl into and out of one another. It's as if her head lies on the pillow next to mine. It doesn't take long before I feel aroused; she's touching me, holding me, exploring me.

"Alison," I say.

She doesn't say anything for a moment. "It's okay. I'm in you. I'm with you," she says.

"It's as if we are one." I feel her retract a little.

"You'd never do anything to hurt me would you?" she says.

I pause—maybe a beat too long.

"Listen," she says, "you need to decide what you want."

"I want you."

"No, really. You can't have it both ways." And then she goes silent.

I no longer sense her presence.

* * *

Tuesday. Alison's voice seems distant, and I wonder if she's still angry with me for allowing the psychiatrist into my apartment. I open the curtains, clean the kitchen—everything to ensure the apartment looks just so, in case of any unanticipated visits. I consider the merits of smoking to help me to relax. I flick

78

through the dictionary from the shared library downstairs but pay it barely any attention. I find myself pacing my room until the early hours of the morning. I pull up a chair close to the television, comb my hand across my hair, and stare into the silver screen. I wait. I listen. I bide my time.

* * *

Friday. Further silence. I distract myself with a walk around the lake. Picking up a slice of stale bread from the kitchen on the way out for the ducks, I step out into the cold morning air. Listening to the shrill voices from the playground, I breathe in the fresh grass clippings around me. As I approach the water by the far side of the lake, I see the dark swan in the reeds, his head deep in the water. With my heart in my mouth, I reach for my pocket, take the small canister of tablets, and open the lid. Tablet by tablet, I drop four of them into the water.

"You should pour them all away."

"So, you are here," I say.

"I was always here."

"You hid on purpose."

"You let her come into the apartment on purpose."

I place a tablet on my tongue.

"What the fucking fuck," she says.

I close my lips around it. "I'm not threatening you–I'm self-medicating."

"You're what?"

"I'm managing my dosage."

"Swallow that tablet," she says, "and I'm gone."

"You have to trust..."

"Trust you—how? Who was it who got you through all those years at the hospital? Who was it who kept you going when you were at your lowest ebb? You either quit with the medication or you don't."

"I didn't create this situation."

"Oh, sure."

"You're impossible," she says. "There's no talking to you when you're in this mood."

"You. You're the reason I'm in this mess." I bite down on the tablet.

"Go ahead. Take the whole lot. See if I care."

* * *

Days pass. We're locked between bouts of extended silence. Alison has become a dull ache on my heart, my frustration simmering somewhere between melancholy and madness.

"Seems you have a decision to make," she says.

"I don't know what to do."

"You have to be honest with yourself."

"You know what I want," I say.

"Yes. But do you?"

* * *

On quieter days I spend long periods outdoors. I venture one bus stop further away at a time. To the lake. To the crematorium. To the post office. I find myself cashing in my weekly cheque for cough candies and butterscotch, bullseyes, and toffees, whole quarter-pound bags stretching the pockets of my anorak. I avoid eye contact with the post office assistant behind the counter.

"A quarter-pound of liquorice-flavoured toffee please," I say.

"You didn't pay last week," she says.

"I'll pay you Saturday when I get my allowance."

"This isn't a charity I'm running."

I step away slowly from the counter while maintaining eye contact with the woman. I exit the post office, stepping past a homeless man in the next doorway, a former outpatient who quit our facility a month back.

* * *

Monday morning. I'm in my bathroom attempting to tidy up the beginnings of a beard as a distraction from the patchiness on top. As I reach for the canister on the shelf, I open the lid and pour the last tablet into my palm. Looking up at my reflection in the mirror I see the faint glow of Alison looking back at me.

"Well?" she says.

I feel the hurt rising from within. "I made my decision."

"It doesn't matter anymore."

"It should."

"No," she says, "nothing matters anymore."

"You're being overdramatic."

"You're not listening to me," she says.

"I don't understand."

"I need you to end all this for me."

"But I..."

"You mock our love with your quetiapine and those weekly tête-à-têtes."

"Look," I say, holding out the empty canister. "Nothing there, see."

"Oh, I see alright," she says.

"I'd do anything for you."

"Good, then you'll take me to the roof, and you'll end it." She begins sobbing.

"But I've given up," I say.

"Then we're both in agreement.

I feel like I've lost everything. I leave the cabinet door hanging open. I drop the empty canister to the floor. I hear Alison crying in the distance.

* * *

Moments later I'm on the flat roof to the apartments. Sprawled out before me I see the auxiliary nurse from reception. She lies in the sun lounger, her huge mass bulging from the distressed material, fold upon fold of flesh bursting the seams. She drops her book and looks my way.

"Lovely day to be out," she says.

I look around the edge of the rooftop and study the raised safety railings.

"Ever read Aesop's fables?" she asks.

All I can see is the sugar on her lips, glistening in the sun like pink liquorice swirls.

"Did you know a swan only sings when it knows that it's about to die?" She reaches down to her side and produces a paper bag. "Donut?"

"How would a swan know that?"

She raises her book. "A man saw a swan in the market and took it home with him. A few days later he has some friends over for dinner and asks the swan to sing, but the swan stays silent. Years pass. When the swan grows old, it becomes aware of its demise and breaks into a sweet, sad song. When its owner hears this, he says if this is the only time it sings, he should have cooked up swan stew a year ago." The nurse closes the book and smiles.

"What's that supposed to mean?" I ask.

"You're sure you won't have a donut?"

"I don't get it," I say.

"Do you like to sing?" The nurse slides her vast swathe of tongue over her teeth. As I turn to leave, she dips her hand back into the bag for another donut.

* * *

An hour later I'm back outside the post office. I spend the next ten minutes pretending to look at wanted ads in the window. I avoid the homeless guy's glare as he pulls the sleeping bag over himself. In the window, I see landscapers, handymen, and an image of a lost dog called Bob. The handwriting next to the name and phone number scrawled in an 'I do not want this dog back' kind of way. I see the post office lady pouring humbugs into a glass jar.

She comes to the doorway with folded arms. "That's five pounds you owe me now."

I hand the woman a screwed up ten-pound note. She takes a step backward to let me in.

"A half-pound of Bullseyes," I say, "with a Curly Wurly and a Twix for the nurse." I pay the woman and tuck the paper bag of sweets into my pocket. As I exit her shop, I drop the chocolate bar onto the sleeping bag.

* * *

That evening I'm back in my room, staring out at a fingernail of moon. Powder-white clouds reflect up from the water, framed by a vast pool of blackness. A sour taste rises like salted liquorice and sinks back down into my stomach. I cough. I spit. I close the window to shut out the noise from the street below. Entering my bathroom, I squeeze out the last of the toothpaste onto my brush. As I turn to switch on the light, I catch Alison staring back at me from the mirror.

"Hey—what's this?" Alison says, "So, we're not talking now." Placing her toothbrush down she begins to apply moisturiser to her forehead. She notices me brushing my hair to the side to cover the patches. "Listen, I see why this place means so much to you. And I get it with the whole tablet thing, I really do. I'm sorry if I made it harder for you."

I watch her rub the cream into her cheekbones. "At the end of the day, you're just a number to her. You've got to keep that in mind if you want to play her at her own game. First, we need to tidy up that hair—let's shave it."

* * *

Alison and I are sitting by the window. The rush hour traffic has died down, and only a lone walker circles the lake. His dog rushes back and forth along the reeds with only its tail in view as it closes in on something.

"I've been thinking," Alison says, "you need to move on from here. This place is full of all the wrong people. With that woman coming and going as she pleases; this situation just isn't good for you. The stress—it's all too much."

I'm nodding. I'm taking all this in.

"You need a fresh start," she says. "That guy living by the post office, he's got the right idea. You want a place you can call you own, somewhere you can get a bit more 'me time' in too."

I hear what she's saying. And while I realise the practicalities of not having a job to support making a move, see the benefits of getting away from this place. It's one thing to move away from the psychiatric hospital, but it's another to release myself from the constant supervision. I think about the possibilities. I imagine a carefree life filled with newfound freedom. I picture a future with just the two of us alone—to finally be free.

* * *

At 7:00 a.m. I wake to the sound of loud banging on the door. I rise from my slumber and step up to the glass window in the door.

"Hello?" I say to the blurred shape. My tired eyes don't recognise her face.

"It's Dr Griffiths. The head supervisor from the hospital."

I respond with silence.

"I'll get to the point. The team and I are worried about you."

"I'm fine, Doctor," I say.

"The psychiatrist says you're not sticking to the correct dosage."

"I'm fine." I hear the tremor in my voice.

"Can you let me in?" She tests the door handle.

I feel myself scratching my hands over my scalp and place both palms on the door.

"I'm afraid we're going to have to look at other options for you," she says.

"He says he's fine, Doctor." I feel my forehead slamming back and forth against the glass.

"Am I speaking to Alison?" the supervisor asks.

"You need to leave him alone," Alison says.

"Robert, you must let me in."

The blood from my forehead blinds my vision. I hear the supervisor fumbling for her keys.

"No," Alison screams, "you're not listening."

"We…we need to help you pack your things."

I hear the raised voices, but none of their words make sense anymore. It's just a garbled back and forth between Alison and the head supervisor. Sounds continue folding into themselves. Light becomes darkness. I'm descending into that warm, cosy place, deep inside—a back-to-the-womb kind of thing, looking for sanctuary. I've been biding my time, waiting to escape. I've been patient for all this time.

- Huddlestone Phillips

84

ICARUS

When my brother fell, I was in the middle of a full time job,
      and a romance,
with a plane ticket to Paris for the weekend.
So five days after hiring a lawyer for him, I got on an airplane,
      numb and in a daze.
While sitting on the back of my boyfriend's motorcycle roaring
      away from the airport,
I tried to figure out why my brother did it.
Was it love, lust, needing to control,
grief, shock, or a story he believed?
Was it the inevitable legacy of our Dad's condemnation
hurled at the youngest of his eight children
      "You are good for nothing!"

Yes, he loved her. Yes, they had lived together. Yes, he took
      care of her.
He had never imagined a day without the woman he thought
      of as his wife.
But she had been unfaithful, and he was overcome.
He got into a space where rules don't exist.
Where the logical mind turns off. Where he couldn't step back.
Or see any more possibilities. Only raw wretched rage.
      And revenge.

Then he fell from the sky, from conscience and consciousness,
and fell from all of our lives - now drowning in the ocean, in
righteousness, in regret, in disgrace, in prison.

- Anne Casapini

The Courtyard

It was my first trip back. I was only ten years old, a child, when I left for America with my brother and mother. Daddy had left six months earlier to look for a job and settle down before our arrival. I didn't return to Delhi until the age of twenty. There had been little communication in those ten years when international phone calls were expensive and reserved for weddings and funerals.

While I had grown in those intervening years, my memories had not. They were as well-maintained, tidy, boxed, and gated as the courtyard of our family house that I remembered, where I had played our version of hopscotch with my brother and cousins. Those memories were as sweet as the sugar cane juice that we devoured as a regular treat from the cart in the crowded market just one house away. Sometimes the Juicewalla wheeled his trolley onto our street, passing directly in front of our house, yelling, "Cold, cold, sugar cane juice, come and get it," at the top of his voice. We could hear it in the bedrooms and even in the back courtyard that had a door leading into the alley, where my grandmother, Mataji, often sat hand-churning butter in a wooden mechanism made for that purpose, or cutting green beans, or peeling potatoes into a bucket of water to keep them from browning.

Hearing that call, we ran to any of my three uncles, all younger to Daddy, or my aunts, all living as a joint family in the house, to ask for money for the juice, and, often, they came to the street with us. Together we watched as the Juicewalla pushed the sugar cane into the steel machine, watched the foamy cream-colored liquid fill the waiting glasses, saw him mix in salt and spices before giving it to us to gulp down.

My memories were chip-free, unlike the flaking iron gate that marked the entry to the courtyard. My cousin Seema and I used to stand on the bottom rung holding on to the iron bars, blissfully indifferent to the reprimand that was sure to follow from all the elders of the house. I stood on the gate and pushed with my feet to swing it open or closed, feeling the air rushing through my hair, against my face. Our constant weight took the gate hinges out of alignment. The elders of the house could all scold me, but only my mother could slap my tender cheeks when I did something wrong. Her slaps were usually from impatience, she had work to do and my nonadherence to rules took time away from her chores. Even then, I rubbed the redness and ran, undaunted, to continue playing. From the small airplane window, I looked into the ocean below.

* * *

"Let's go swimming."

Seema and I let the water run in the bathroom. There was no tub, only the bare floor with a drain that we clogged with a nearby rag. Once the water rose to one inch we lay on our tummies, arms pretend splashing, clothed only in underwear, imagining ourselves in deep waters until our mothers called. Other people needed to use the only bathroom in the house. Neither one of us had ever seen a pool.

In the crowded market, Uncle Umi's hand held mine fast. We walked to the market towards the throng gathered in front of Radha's Saris and Shawls. Uncle lifted me to his shoulders, and I craned my neck. There was a black box in the glass window. The screen faced the street on which images danced like in a movie. Someone had put a movie into a black box.

* * *

I looked at my mother and father sitting next to me sleeping in the cramped airplane seats, going home, looking forward to meeting parents, brothers, sisters. We all had done this journey before, the initial crossing of the ocean to get to America. After the long, long voyage that seemed to never end, we had entered Uncle Tar's house in Encino, California for the first time. It opened into a large living room, in the corner of which stood a black box.

I gasped. It was true. They had a private television inside their own house, on a stand in the corner of the living room. I was compelled somehow to look past the box and through the sliding glass doors and saw a gleaming pool of sapphire water.

What will I say to her, my best childhood friend, my sister with whom I spent my best summers, either at our house or hers, while our mothers, real sisters, chatted away with hot tea and biscuits between them, with whom I swam in one inch of water? Will I tell her that my Uncle Tar has a pool in the backyard of his house and that his wife, my aunt, has taught me how to swim? Will I tell her how I ached for her with every new experience in those initial years, desperate to share with her the after-school unsupervised play in the school yard with a new friend, golden-haired Lisa?

Lisa and I, both tall for our age and lanky, ran to the rings as soon as the bell rang, to the rings that let me fly much, much higher and faster than the gate to the courtyard, and much, much longer, as long as I could catch the next ring without falling, the rings that habitually bruised my palms and hers with blood red blisters so much so that we were both regularly sent to the nurse's office by our sixth grade teacher who was shaken by our wounds.

Will I share with her my victories in vocabulary tests, English vocabulary tests, that I aced in spite of being the 'foreigner'? Will I tell her my defeats, about the baseball bat thrust into my hands as I followed the running students into the field during recess? They were excited about the new kid then and they bade me stand in a spot, they let me go first, and suddenly there was something in my hands that looked like a cricket bat, but was not, and a ball was coming at my face really fast. Cricket was for boys, and I had never held a cricket bat either. I dodged the baseball until someone told me to hit it. My feeble attempts to connect with the round white sphere that was hurtling towards me were futile and I saw the sheer disappointment in the faces of my new American classmates.

From then on, I became the girl who was picked last for any sports teams and then only because there was no other choice. I, who had been schooled in classical dance, high jump, sewing, and disciplined marching. Left, left…left, right left. I was not schooled to keep my eye on the ball until it connected, booming that perfect thud with the baseball bat.

Will I tell her how much I pained for her, for our sisterhood?

Will I share my pain when my classmates told me that I should not wear fishnet stockings to the elementary school graduation because my dark skin would show through?

* * *

It was the middle of the night when we landed, unfurled, and stretched as we exited the plane, holding our heavy carry-ons. As soon as my tennis-shoe-clad feet left the plane, I was hit by the hot air as if from a volcano. I thought someone had left the heater on, but we were just outside in high summer. Even at two in the morning, the temperature was heavy, sweaty, suffocating.

One of my uncles had come to receive my father, their elder brother, and take us back to the family home. My memories ran wild as we turned into the narrow dark street where our house was located. I didn't remember the cars, so many parked on both sides leaving hardly any room for our van to maneuver. I thought, *there will be a park now, the one with the surrounding fence where we played*, and there it was, serene and quiet in the dead of night. And, finally, I was face to face with the gate, still chipped ten years later. The courtyard was littered with images that flooded, the hopscotch, the hide and seek. It was much smaller than I remembered it to be, even though this play area had already been curtailed before my departure by the addition of a room.

I was oblivious to the joyful assembly happening around me, food and drink being offered in Daddy's honor and his due respect as the elder, even though it was so late. In the dim light, I could still see that the wooden cane chairs were the very same as in my childhood, well-used and unstaining, with fresh holes in the crisscross of the caning. Everyone seemed to be wearing faded dull-colored clothes, the color of dust. In my hand, I still clutched the small wings the airline stewardess had given me as we deplaned. My palms hurt from the sharp points of the metal. The noise had fallen away.

I looked around for Seema. Directed to the bedroom, I saw her, long-haired, sitting on the bed with an elaborately embroidered shawl draped over her like a blanket. Anxious to reconnect I went to meet her, standing in the doorway, smiling expectantly. It was the open-hearted, big, American smile, one that invited easily to share in apple pies, white picket fences, and candy canes. It was the smile of our lost childhood together, of lost time, and tearful goodbyes.

Her returned smile was not as sincere as mine. It was restrained and reserved, embedded in the culture of conservatism, where self-control and limitations are fed, grown, nurtured. It was not full of our memories of hide-and-seek that I had lived on for the past ten years. Her smile didn't seek to remember our chases, shared baths, forced naps, and unreserved laughter. It didn't look for more in me, to rewire, relink, and rejoin.

I had been plucked out of that life at a tender age, but I had stayed there, glued to the images of a ten-year-old, still connected to a child's unconditional feeling of friendship and love for a beloved sister.

I tried again to regain my childhood friend and sat on the edge of the bed, facing her. With this view, I could see that her belly was swollen and that she was with child. I had not grown full my feathers and she was flying, married and with child.

An ocean had separated us for ten long formative years. Although we sat together at last, I saw that the deep sea that I had just crossed was still there on the hard Indian style bed, between us, dividing us, born of culture and schooling and the way of our own separate villages.

Seema had moved on.

- Renu Chopra

90

Catch and Release

The river was running faster this spring than ever, evidenced by the monstrous roar from the gorge above the bend. Canyon walls reverberated with the din. Furious currents roller-coastered over and around sharp rocks with tufts of slippery moss to-ing and fro-ing in the merciless churn. I was standing in the middle of it all, wavering in one of the slower-moving eddies when a silver flash slapped against my waders: a gut-hooked rainbow trout.

Robert was situated a stone's throw up-current beside a jutting knife of granite, surprised by the snagged fish on his line. Footing unsteady, he fought to stay upright amid the aquatic rage. It was a dicey place to fish. We shouldn't have been there. I'd picked the spot.

Gut-hooked. That's how I felt over morning coffee at the campsite when Robert admitted I was right. He'd been sleeping with someone who didn't mean a thing to him. That's what he said. "So what? No big deal. Didn't mean a thing to me."

"It's alright," I said. "We'll get through it."

I tucked the grip of my rod under my arm, eased down to feel for the line and scooped the thrashing trout out of the chill mountain water. Silver, green and red with dark spots, it was a hefty lunker, but I was angry Robert had used a treble hook with three sharp points rather than a single hook; a single hook being the choice of any responsible angler because it's more sporting and does minimal damage to the animal's flesh. It's an important consideration, allowing a person to release under-sized juveniles unharmed, or any fish for that matter. It's called catch and release, freeing the animal to live another day. The treble hook explained why the trout was so easily snagged.

I shook my head as I carefully extracted two of the barbed points that had bitten deep into the belly of the poor thing. Robert grinned and gave me a thumbs up when I at last freed the wriggling prey, but rather than putting it in my creel as he expected, I flipped the rainbow back into the river.

It rolled awkwardly as the rapids swept it downstream and I could tell the wound was mortal.

Peeved I'd released his catch rather than kept it for dinner, Robert gave me an angry "what's up with that?" gesture. I shrugged and gave a little tug on the line I still held. It didn't take much, just enough to put him off balance. I think he hit his head on something. He reminded me of the trout when he floated by. Funny, from that moment on he didn't mean a thing to me.

Geoffrey Graves

I Would Like to Speak to the Manager of the Ghost Factory

I want to complain about my ghost. He's shit. I'm sorry, but that's what he is. When I bought my house – it's an old house, one of those big Greek Revival ones on the outskirts – I said, *you know what this place needs? A ghost.* I told that to my partner, and she was in total agreement. It adds a certain *je ne sais quoi.* I'm not sure what that is, but a ghost would certainly add it. And who hasn't wanted to have one's friends over for the first time and coyly confess that *yes, this place is haunted?*

He was in your catalog. My partner and I sat together on the chaise longue after we'd put our daughter to bed. I scrolled through the iPad. She refilled our drinks, and maybe we were just a little bit tipsy but not so much that we weren't being selective. The ghost we picked was clearly – *clearly* – advertised as your "premium stock." You wrote – no, listen, I went back and copied it out – you wrote *locally sourced and independently verified, phantoms of the highest caliber, each specter is cultivated from the most prestigious selection of lost souls and is guaranteed* – gaur-an-teed – *to bring elegance and historicity to* –

Please, will you let me finish?

We picked our ghost from that list.

What?

The serial number?

No, I don't have it. You know which one it was. It was the one that did the murders.

What?

I don't know. It was the eighteenth century. Or nineteenth century. Whichever one of those means the 1800s. *I said I don't know.* It was the one that looked like a mortician mixed with an undertaker. The one that came in the box packed with sawdust. It had a mason jar inside. Black glass that smelled of bergamot and nutmeg. It doesn't matter if the number's written on the tag inside, we wound up throwing it away. You should have a record of these things.

Sorry. I'm tired.

He was good for the first few nights. My partner and I were woken up by the sound of footsteps on the floor above us. The long, tortured creaking of the stairs made us shiver with delight. Our daughter fled to our room, practically shaking. We took turns holding her, telling her it was alright, to think how thrilling it was.

He was a moaner. Nothing *petite* about that *mort*. In the dead blankness before dawn, the hallways trembled with his agonized howl. It was the type you could feel in the roots of your molars. We were so excited to show him off. We'd just finished redecorating the garden and we're on the cusp of picking the theme for the housewarming party when it all went horribly wrong.

Three days. That's how long he lasted for. Three days.

I was finishing the calligraphy on the seating cards when I heard our daughter screeching. She'd been on edge ever since we got the ghost, but this was twisted with urgency. I ran up the stairs to her room, arriving just a second ahead of my partner. Our daughter was standing on her bed, shoving herself into a corner, pointing at something in the carpet.

It was this moon-white dome, floating through the fibers. This sort of pearlescent bubble that moved one direction and then another like a spectral Roomba. My partner got up on the bed with our daughter, trying to calm her down but I rushed downstairs to the pantry, where I saw the ghost's legs protruding from the ceiling and dangling through the cans of baked beans.

I'm saying he was floating at the wrong altitude. I want that notated, OK? *Floating. At. Wrong. Height.*

Tell me this: does it bring *elegance* and *historicity* to be menaced by a pair of size eleven wingtips at one in the morning? Would you feel haunted if you rolled a bar cart through a mass murderer's forehead in the middle of a thunderstorm, and he didn't even notice?

Excuse me, does it sound like I'm even *close* to being

94

done?

Floating wrong was just the start of it. He's showing up during the day.

I don't mean at sunset, when the shadows are long and crooked, or on a grim, overcast day when the clouds soak up the light like a leper's bandages. I mean he's been materializing at ten o'clock on a bright, sunny morning – shuffling morosely through my term papers or sulking crotch-high in the middle of the charcuterie table.

It's not just off-putting, it's distinctly un-menacing. If you see a man in eighteenth, nineteenth, oh my god, *whatever* attire, you expect to be disconcerted. You're supposed to hear the *l'appel du vide* and feel the glorious grotesquery of the moment wash over you. When it's gone (the ghost, the moment), you feel invigorated. Revitalized. Like those ice baths at that resort in Denmark my partner and I go to. *This* is not a cold shower. *This* is not a Nordic cascade. *This* is a drippy faucet. A constant presence. A quality ghost is like a quality waiter – only ever there when you need him. *Your* ghost doesn't vanish, he just hovers there, sometimes for hours. This isn't what we paid for.

No. Do not put me on hold. I do not want to be transferred to another department. I want you to do something about it. He's started bringing in trash.

Ghosts are supposed to fling books off shelves, slam doors, flicker lights, and stack chairs on tables in disquieting ziggurats. They're supposed to write *GET OUT* in blood on the walls of the foyer. Ghosts are not supposed to leave seashells around the house. We don't even know where's he's getting them. Ghosts are not supposed to write HELLO and MY NAME IS JOSIA and I SINCERELY HOPE YOU HAVE A LOVELY DAY in piles of dust on the patio tiles. They're not supposed to leave kittens in your daughter's playroom. She says it's only been once, but I *know* she's hiding more. I have allergies. I can tell.

You see how unacceptable it's gotten. Not even *she's* afraid of him, and they'd hanged him for being a child-killer.

He's a bad influence. A few weeks ago, I found our

daughter had used my partner's oil paints to scrawl MY
NAME IS CLAUDINE on the wall of the upstairs hallway.
She's lying to me about the kittens. She's got an entire coven
of them somewhere. The ensuite of the guest room reeks –
reeks – of cat piss. She's become such a little monster lately.
I'm sure she knows the whereabouts of the black mason jar
but she just isn't telling us.

Obviously, we tried fixing it ourselves. I've been
spending days on the phone, *calling* and *calling* people, and
nobody wants to help. I asked the store, and the store said I
had to talk to quality control, and quality control said they
were sorry but I'd have to talk to the store. Whatever happened to personal responsibility? Can you tell me? Meanwhile, my daughter is floating around the house, carried by
invisible hands that never tire, her hair brushed and braided
by fingers that've arranged the locks on god-knows-how-
many corpses. And my partner's been trying to research it
herself. That's right. She's barricaded herself in the study, not
sleeping, barely eating, just reading through old newspapers
and documents. Last week, she staggered downstairs in the
middle of a *soiree*, looking like the living-dead, standing in
the kitchen with the fridge door open, eating pickles out of a
jar while our guests all gawked and stared. I've never been so
mortified in my life. I had to tell them it was a side effect of
her diet pills. I had to practically drag her upstairs, and when
I was helping her to bed, do you know what she told me?
She says, *There's a chance the man they hanged wasn't even
responsible for all those missing children.*

You know what I call that?

I call that a rip-off.

Blatant false advertising.

Deceptive, misleading *horseshit*. What are you people
even doing up there? I want to know. I want –

For God's sake, here he is now. Yes, the ghost, who do
you think I've been talking about this whole time?

I said I did not want to be transferred.

I don't know – he's just standing there. He's knee-deep
in the floor with his back to me. I'm snapping my fingers at

96

him but he's not turning around. And oh, there he goes –
back down into the floor, right on cue. Would you put up
with this sorry display?

I AM NOT OVERREACTING.

Last week, my partner started hanging pictures
in her study. Not as in "hanging framed artistic photos of
abandoned bedframes." As in "thumbtacking illustrations of
long-dead children right into the wall." As in "running red
thread between grainy photocopies of old obituary clippings
to pins on a map of Connecticut." As in "spending hours
talking to wheezy local historians while dinner gets cold and
our daughter pockets scraps to feed to those goddamned cats
that I can *hear* and *smell* but can't ever *find*."
Why won't anyone *help*?

It can't go on. We both know where this is headed. I
can practically *smell* it now.

The mixed odor of our bodies as we cram into the
car, plunging eastward across the continent. I'll have to do
all the driving. Hours and hours of it. My partner will still
be pouring through her antique maps, chewing on repulsive
gas-station pork rinds, trying to decipher the location of
this ancient farmhouse or *that* weatherworn headstone. Our
daughter will be in the back, clutching the black glass mason
jar to her belly, which she'll confess to having hidden some-
place infuriatingly obvious. We'll probably be somewhere
past Santa Fe – too far to turn back – when I'll start sniffling
and realize she's brought a kitten too.

Understand where I'm coming from. *Please.*

I don't want to stagger into neon-lit motels where the
sheets are heavy from decades of dead skin cells. I don't want
to eat at roadside diners where blue-haired women call you
"hon." I don't want to encounter a sequence of colorful characters in some decaying town where we try to clear the name
of some soul who's already dead, who's been dead for over a
century, who isn't even *good* at being dead.

It's not fair.

I have grading to do. My partner has her showing at
our friend's gallery, and she's already rescheduled twice. Our

daughter is supposed to be taking language lessons right now and we were all going to Copenhagen in August. None of this is our fault. We shouldn't be getting punished for it.

Help *me* help *you* help *me*, alright? I want to talk to someone. I need to talk to someone who's in charge. Don't tell me they're in a meeting. No. No. No. I am not leaving until I speak to someone. I will stay on this line all day if I have to. I will stay on this line forever. I'll wither up and die and get scooped up into a jar by your techs and mislabeled and I will haunt *you* just to show you how to do it properly, do you hear me? I'll do it. I swear that – ah, *finally*! Yes, I want to lodge a complaint.

- Gordon Brown

Cassandra with the Lilac Tongue

Remember me? Cassandra? But you always call me
Cassie, she says.

When he opened his eyes, he'd found her there,
sitting on his bed beside him. Was she there all night,
or did she arrive at dawn? He's never seen her before,
he's sure, though she acts as if they are more than acquaintances.

She has a ring on every finger. And her tongue—
she keeps flicking it along her lips—it looks
as if she dyed it purple.

I'm here to tell you, darling, I'm pregnant.
Pregnant, she says, stroking her swollen belly
as if showing him where, *with a small farm, a cistern,*
rocky fields, an olive grove, three goats, six chickens,
and a dozen children. And they're yours.
All of them, my love, yours.

He looks up at the Madonna on the wall.
She seems to lower her eyes, which makes him feel
even more confused.

Would you like something to drink? Cassandra asks.
He doesn't know what to say. His tongue feels like a bat
scorched by the sun. She goes over to the table,
picks up the bottle of ouzo, and pours it into the glass
left there from last night. He takes a sip and hears himself sigh.

Outside the window, he can see a man in a black-visored cap
standing near the tree stump. He seems at ease,
yet waiting for something to happen.

She holds out an open hand, as if telling him,
Examine this carefully. Your life might depend on it.

He gazes into her palm, and then, not knowing
what else to do, he kisses it.

Don't worry, she says. *I'll take care of everything.*

                                        - John Bradley

My Mother's Memory Becomes a Pantoum

My fingers as a child played piano on the table.
Mickey could play any song without reading music.
The nice neighbor lady, she'll turn on my sprinkler.
That lower branch in the blue spruce, it looks brown.

Mickey could play by ear but never liked music.
Joan gets my groceries when she buys her groceries.
That brown branch in the blue spruce, I can see it.
The car won't start, but I don't bother with it now.

Joan calls me when she needs to get groceries.
Rod won't wear a mask when he works anywhere.
My car won't start, but then where am I going.
My father bought the piano for me, not my mother.

Rod, under the sink yelling—I just let him curse.
Remember that window over the front door?
My own mother, she was jealous of me getting a piano.
The neighbors on both sides will soon be gone.

That window over the front door keeps fogging over.
On the kitchen table, my fingers playing the piano.
Both neighbors gone all winter—I don't like it.
Now, I didn't tell you this story already, did I?

- John Bradley

THE ROOSTER AND THE PIG

Work let out late, again. And we all wandered down to *The Rooster and The Pig*. Again. A well-worn walk for anyone who works the Barcelona waterfront and a Friday night grab-ass for all the sots of the shipyard: the buff stevedores, those smelly apes just off the sardine boats, the harbor pilots in their fucking white hats, the British swabbies from that damn submarine that has been crowding the outer harbor for the last four days, and marine techs like me . . . and Duffy . . . and the new kid. They brought me here light-years ago as some kinda initiation after my first week with *Tecnologies Marines de Barcelona*—the week that most squids get fired. I've been here every Friday ever since. Unless I'm off rebuilding a drydock in the Seychelles or trying to keep a two-hundred-year-old embarkation pier from sliding into the Persian Gulf. For the fifth time. Loud and smelly as a boys' locker room after a game being in this place is part of my job; a good place to find out who's shipping out and who's back in town. Still, I never want to see either of my own sons in a fucking place like this.

"Ei, Lex, you son-of-a-bitch! Drag your sorry ass on over here!"

To make room Duffy shoves the new kid with the Team Barça cap off of the barstool next to him. A nod to the barman gets a quick Estrella Damm sliding down my way, its soapy head slopping down the side of the mug.

Team Barça kid worms his way back into the space between me and Duffy. Standing now, he's waving at the barman trying get a beer slid down his way. Yeah, I know his story. Same as mine. Hot-shit, small-town fútbol hero comes down to Barcelona with a dream of playing in the big leagues. No chance. Got himself a job on the waterfront, put in with Duffy and me, lasted the first week now he's jostling for a spot at the *The Rooster and The Pig*. Another twenty years of this shit and he'll have his drink sliding down the bar as soon as he walks through the door. Yeah. It'll take twenty years for this kid.

Off my starboard shoulder a big-haired, Godzilla of

a dame mushrooms over a barstool while three horny swabs take turns trying to sit on her lap. She could eat them all in one bite if she wanted to.

"No! That's why they get 'em tattooed on their feet," a swab was bawling at her.

"On their feet?" She crinkles her false eyelashes. "Why, that must hurt."

"Oh yes, Madonna. Gotta be on the feet."

"So, you float that way when your boat goes down," another pipes in.

"Ya' float feet up."

"Rooster on one foot. Pig on the other."

"But doesn't that hurt? I mean one's foot is a very sensitive part of one's body."

"Oh, baby. I got lots of sensitive parts." The swabbie is grabbing at his crotch. "ya' just gotta go looking for 'em."

Somehow that is hysterical to them.

Back on my port side the new kid gets his beer and he's all grinning like an idiot just to be one of the boyos. I chink my mug against his. "Good luck, kid."

Duffy is half turned away from me yakking with some other guys we'd been workin' with. He rolls around towards me and scowls down at my mug.

"Oh, come on now, Lex," he bitches. "Ya' goin' soft on me, mate."

A hand signal to the barman and two shot glasses filled with . . . something . . . come sliding our way. We hook each other's arms, simultaneously toss back the smokey liquid and slam the empties down on the bar with a hard cack. Duffy turns back to his yammering coterie while I wince to the all-to-familiar rush that is eating away at my brain.

"Ain't that right, Lex?" One of the swabs is shouting at me. "Roosters and pigs."

"What about 'em?" The guy is going in and out of focus.

The lady seems to be undulating on her stool.

"It's a fact, ain't it. Roosters and pigs keep floating when your ship goes down. Tell her, Lex. She'll believe you."

I shake my head and just say "fuck you."

Even with his back turned I can hear Duffy's raspy, bull-horn of a voice above the din. ". . . ya' might say that but in some place it's still okay to kill your wife. We knew a guy down in Chile . . ." he cranks his head back towards me, ". . . didn't we, Lex?" then back to his audience, ". . . strangled his wife. Went right down and told the policía after and, just like that, they said they didn't get involved in family matters. The guy's still workin' his job. Goin' to Church and all."

"Bullshit."

"True as I'm standing here."

"You're sitting."

A clamor of mushed together sounds pulsed in waves. I couldn't make much out of it. But I worked that job down in Chile with Duffy and I didn't hear nothin' like that.

"Sure. Claimed to be screwing one of our guys." Bit of Duffy's voice roll over the hullabaloo. "Na! Don't know who." Came in pieces. "But that poor gal, she's a dead 'un now."

Words aren't falling together for me but I feel the blade-edge of his tongue slice through my abdomen and scrape across my bowels. Puke rises in the back of my throat. It has the taste of seasickness but it is running through me like terror.

I lunge past Team Barça kid, beer going all down his shirt, and grab the arm of Duffy's jacket. "Where the fuck did you hear that?"

"Ya' wanna let go of my jacket, Lex?" Everything goes still when Duffy stares me down. "Or ya' want me to break your fuckin' arm off?"

I let go. Back off. "That Punta Arenas job? Where did you get that shit?"

A brain piercing screech rips across the room. Some sailor with a Goddamn saxophone is trying to play along with the juke box. A painful noise but hoots and cheers surge through the joint egg him on.

"Who's the guy?"

He squares off to me. "The wife-killing guy? I don't know who the fuck he was. I just heard about it from the purs-

104

er." Then his face reshapes itself into a half-moon grin. "What? Lex, my man. You the dog who poked her?"

Oh, they are all rolling with that one. Even the swabbies behind me and that beer-drenched Team Barça kid, all howling at that.

They all make me sick. It's all spinning. Going in and out. Turning away from those assholes I find a shot glass sitting on the bar—something the swabbies couldn't finish. While reaching for it I notice my hands quivering. That rage is coming back. Down the hatch, I either say or thought as some awful spirit burns out the back of my throat.

"Hey, mate!" One of 'em comes off the fat lady's lap. "That was mine!"

I remember punching him in the face. That's all I remember.

* * *

Home again somehow. Sprawled across my bed, boots and all, like I'd been dropped there. Waiting for the room to stop heaving about and hold still and my brains to stop pounding on my skull. The water running in the toilet bowl is driving me bat-ass crazy. Whoever flushed it last didn't know to hold the handle all the way down. That's where I see my face for the first time. "Oh, God." Someone got me good.

Time to pull myself together. Way past time. And it's gonna take more than this handful of Tylenol Extra Strength. I get some water and sit on the edge of the bed trying to push back against this gusher of shit that I don't really want to know about.

I have my old tried-and-true when I'm this way. I dig out my phone and dial up my ex.

She still takes my calls any time day or night.

"Oh, Lex. You just missed the boys. Tommy's taking them skiing for the weekend. Picked them up right after school."

Tommy. My sons get to go skiing with Tommy. Wham. A big right hook lays me out again. Should have seen that one coming.

"So, you've got the house to yourself this weekend."

"Rainy weekend, you know," she laughs a little. "Let's see: three males plus a rainy weekend. Hmm? That means that I get to catch up on the housework."

I've tried but I have never been able to work up any anger at Tommy. All around good guy. I never took my boys skiing.

"You out on a job, Lex?"

"No. I've been home port for a while now. Maintenance and repair. Maintenance and repair all day long."

"Oh, then you're caught up in this rain, too?"

"I'll make for good snow up in the mountains."

Not that there really was a dame in every port. But, sure, there were some. No matter where I am, who I might be with I always sleep really good after sex. I know that pisses them off. But that whole thing in Puenta Arenas was different. She really wasn't the messing-around type. More like a nun-on-the-run. This one left me confused and sleepless. *Oh, God!* Now to find out that she'd been laid out. What kind of guy would do that? I put my free hand across my face. *It is absolutely amazing the things that I manage to fuck up!*

"You okay, Lex?" She knows me too well.

"Yeah." I suck in a deep breath that made me cough a little. "Are they getting good at it? Skiing, I mean?"

"They tell me they like it. They got lessons last year. It makes it easy to find Christmas presents for them."

I like to think that my boys will grow up to be the kind of men that don't fuck things up all the time. Maybe they could get that part from Tommy.

Now Duffy's battering his way back into my head and that time me and him were walking a quay in some dumpy little port, the Malacca's if I remember right. Right there in front of us this guy just hauls off and belts his wife. Smack across her face. Knocked her on her ass right there on the quay with other people walking around. I guess it was his wife. I didn't know what that was about. It was just so Goddamn wrong that I started for the guy but Duffy grabbed me and said, "None of our business, mate," and we just walked past like it was all okey. I'm hoping that my kids will grow up to be the kind of men who won't walk just away from shit like that.

"Lex? You there?"

"Yeah. I'm here."

She gives one of those little laughs she uses to cut the tension. "I was afraid we got cut off or something."

"No. No. I'm right here."

"The boys are looking forward to seeing you at Christmas, you know." They only see me at Christmas because she makes them.

"Aw, but honey that's what I was callin' about. I'll be shippin' out over the holidays. Going back to that project in Punta Arenas. We got a weather window down there."

It was an old habit. Even though we'd been divorced forever, I'd still call and tell her when I was shoving off.

"That job down in Chile?"

"That's the one."

"I thought that deal was tied up in a big international law suit. I even saw it on the news. Sounded like we were ready to go to war."

I can picture her in that scolding stance she used on me so often. Even then I thought it was cute and look where it got us. And that girl in Punta Arenas is dead because of me.

"The last thing you told me was that you'd get arrested if you or anyone from *Tecnologies Marines* set foot in Punta Arenas again."

"No. It's okay. I'm going down there to work things out."

"You? Now there *will* be a war. Just don't get yourself thrown in some prison down in Chile, Lex. If not this Christmas the boys are looking forward to seeing you sometime in the future. You are their only father, you know."

Their only father? Well, it's time for their only father to buck up, isn't it? Time to make things right, for once.

We ring off with our usual goodbye that avoids any hints of lingering affection. That call gives me the backbone I need. Not that my company will know anything about it, but I said it out loud. Going to do it. The room is getting a little softer and everything is coming into focus now that I am a man with a purpose.

* * *

Criminals are dumb. That's why they get caught. They get all fixated on the deed and they don't think about the peripherals. Peripherals. At *Tecnologies Marines* they teach us to "focus on the peripherals and the job will fall into place." So, I know to do that.

Figured I'd use a gun. It was South America, right? They all use guns down there. Sure, I know a guy who knows a guy but I'm not going to call him on my phone. The TMB takes me up to Estación de Barcelona-Sants where it is easier to get a prepaid mobile than a post card. I don't go inside the terminal—they got surveillance cameras all over the place. At a kiosk out on the street I get my burner and made my call.

Dealing in firearms is a new skill for me but getting hardware into another country falls right into my area of expertise. Few people know how to remove the steel turning-drum housing on a marine shiplift winch and I am one of them. An unregistered SIG .357 and a few rounds stow neatly in there. By sea it will take a few weeks to get to Punta Arenas. Then it's gonna take a few more months for the paperwork to catch up with the bean counters at Tecnologies Marines. That gives me plenty of time to grow out a nice big beard and catch a flight. After that it will take I don't know how long for someone to figure out that somethings up and by then the job will be done.

* * *

"That beard is quite becoming of you, Senyor Taberner." Bernat doesn't seem at all surprised to find me sitting in his office. Oversized windows face out to the Strait of Magellan, that wicked rant of water that slices the through southernmost tip of Chile. The weather is always miserable here. All you can see out those windows is a steady grey rain and the promise of more to come.

Bernat Ferré is the boss of a gangling ship repair outfit in Punta Arenas. He is also the de facto head of the Catalán expatriate community in Patagonia. It was that connection to Catalunya that landed *Tecnologies Marines de Barcelona* the

108

dock repair contract and brought Duffy and me and the boyos down here. Bernat was the guy who introduced me to her in the first place.

"Cat-er-rina," he said in three distinct beats. She was the hostess of the *Diada de Sant Jordi* costume party that he dragged us to. Married. I saw it on her finger right away. I wasn't the one making the moves.

Now he loafs back in his wire-backed chair and taps on the side of his computer monitor like he's trying to get it to work.

"If our video surveillance system was operating correctly I would have had you arrested at the gate."

"You can still call me Lex, my friend." I speak in Catalán, our common language.

He shakes his head like a disappointed parent.

"The lawsuit is not between you and me, Bernat. It's between a bunch of fucking suits sitting in their fucking glass offices that are about two thousand fucking miles away from here."

A tiny smile creeps into the corners of his mouth. "Our bargaining position would improve greatly if we take you for a hostage."

Ha, ha.

"I brought you a gift."

"Ah, yes. That monstrous chunk of iron that is occupying precious space on my shipping dock. When we saw it was from *Tecnologies Marines* we had to pay a fee to have a bomb squad come by to inspect the contents." He cocks his head. "I am a well-read man, old friend. I know all about the Trojan Horse."

The tone of Bernat's threats set me at ease. "Installing that winch on your pier head was my last task before we got pulled off the job. You need it."

"Take it back." He throws his hands in the air. "Take it back! I don't want it."

"You got a broken-ass dry dock without it."

"No. No! I know how you Spaniards work. You will wait until I have it installed . . ."

"You insult me, Bernat. I am no more Spanish than you."

". . . and then you will send me an invoice . . ."

"We are Catalán, you and I. Brothers. You can trust me."

". . . and we will refuse pay the invoice. Then *Tecnologies Marines* will sue me, a humble expatriate trying to eke out a living down here in the rectum of Chile."

"Trust me, Bernat."

". . . Then we'll have the Trade Councilors down here, again. Arguing with the Minister of Commerce in front of TV cameras, and those Belgian morons from the WTO, again and *ay yi yi.*"

A row of three-ring binders sits behind Bernat's desk, along with clipboards and single sheets of paper taped to the wall: phone numbers, shipping manifests, timetables. Above them a random collection of mementoes and photographs; some black and white, some color. Some in frames but most just stuck up there with push-pins and left to curling at the edges. All of them together made something of a raggedy wreath around a large and particularly unaccomplished painting of a derelict freighter plowing boldly through an unrealistically turquoise-colored ocean. Last time I was here I had offered to replace that hideous painting with something less awful.

Bernat wouldn't have it. "Why that's our glorious ship *Winnipeg*," he told me back then. "The steamship that evacuated our people when Barcelona was falling to Franco in '36."

"Was that one of your daughter's grade school art projects?" I cracked.

I remember how he went all stern on me. "My grandmother was onboard that ship."

Then in a more somber and believable tone. "But I do have a grandmother. And she was on that ship with what was left of her family."

Another photo on that wall grabbed at me. A party shot, in color. *Diada de Sant Jordi.* A triumvirate of men poised in red barrentinas, billowing white shirts and red sashes, the traditional costume of Catalunya. She was standing a half-step

110

in front of them, postcard perfect in a classic pubilla dress.

"Victor Rey, of Llojta de Ray." Bernard points him out for me. "Then me, of course, and Arnau and his wife. We are not elected in a legal sense but we are the go-to men in our community."

The go-to men in the photo are stiff and full of themselves. Quizzically she stares out at me, unbothered by the strands of hair blowing across her cheeks and secretly holding onto the glow of a woman who was, at last, satisfied by a real man—fulfilled but unsmiling as if she knew then how this would end for her.

I'm wondering how she died? Did that asshole husband of hers knife her in her sleep? Or maybe strangle her in the bath tub so he could feel her struggle? And for what? In this picture he looked like the cold, beady-eyed calculating type. One night. That is not a capital offense. Not in a civilized world.

"You introduced me to your friend there in the red Santa hat." I point. "Who did you say that was?"

"Barretina, you mean. Catalonyan's don't wear Santa hats."

"Nobody in Barcelona wears a barretina. Except, maybe, at the tourist shows."

"That is Senyor Didac. Arnau Didac. Good man."

I stare hard at the photo. I hate him.

He went on. "His wife used to be hostess of *Diada de Sant Jordi*. But no more."

Yeah. I heard about that, I kept to myself. "Didn't he work for you? An accountant or something?"

"Arnau? No. Not for me. Senyor Didac is a big man here. Head Prefect over at the Patagonian Herdsman Co-op. He looks after all the wool and mutton that ships out of Punta Arenas."

Arnau Didac. Patagonian Herdsman Co-op. Now I just have to get to the winch that was sitting on Bernat's dock.

"Why do you ask?" Bernat brings me back from my scheming.

"What?"

"About my friend Arnau Didac?"

"This might be a little far-fetched, Bernat, but I was thinking that I could gift my shiplift winch to a friend of yours, like Senyor Didac, there. Then he could make it available to you."

Bernat shook his head and smiled at me. "You think too much like those fucking men in their fucking glass offices, Senyor Taberner."

"Just a thought, my friend. Just a thought."

* * *

The rain squall whipped up into a full-blown gale and the day surrendered to it once again. The lights of the town twinkled in anemic defiance as everyone was pushed inside. The working stiffs in Punta Arenas, I found out, keep their appointments regardless of the weather.

"At this hour? He will be at her grave." His office tells me. "That's where he'll be this evening."

They only got one cemetery here. It isn't hard to find. I walk hunched forward in my oilskin, hat over my ears, fondling the cold steel muzzle of the SIG .357 in my pocket. I'm not thinking about what a big deal this is, I'm just thinking about the cold and that I need to get this fucking chore done before I can get warmed up again. *Cementerio Municipal* sits on the uphill side of town and has a fence all around it. And lots of gates. The ground inside is soggy. Thunder bolts keep me from stumbling over markers. And I find him.

He is a little guy. Has his back to me. Standing in front of a single slant headstone that glistens like a neon sign when the lightning cracks. His left hand steadies an umbrella over his head.

Keeping him in sight I squat against a tree to check my weapon. Four rounds. Chambered the first one. Released the safety. Nobody around. The fierce Patagonian drencher covers my approach.

He's wearing a gentleman's fedora and an overcoat that goes below his knees. Another flash of lightning and the name etched into the marker jumps out: DIDAC. I level the

112

steel blue barrel at the back of his head and call his name.

Nothing.

Nothing but the deluge. A storm so deafening that you could drive a bulldozer between us and he wouldn't have noticed.

I yell it. "Didac!"

He turns slowly and takes a step back when he sees my weapon. Still holding his umbrella. His other hand is cinched around bouquet of store-bought flowers. Yellow, I think. His raises his bouquet hand in surrender. He has a face that is borrowed from a foreign bank note: pompous and contemplative with wire glasses and a neatly trimmed goatee.

He speaks in a slow Latin dialect of Spanish. "I will give you whatever it is you wish, but please, sir, consider the lasting effect that pistol could have on my two young daughters and my wife."

"Your wife!" bursts out of me. "What kind of man can murder his wife and then bring flowers to her grave?"

A sheet of rain rips hard at us, beating at my back and slapping at his face. He doesn't move, but I see his eyes narrow as he says "These flowers are for my mother here." He gestures ever so slightly. "Today is her birthday."

The downpour is beating his flowers to tatters. Water glistens off the blue steel of my SIG .357 and chills my outstretched hand.

"Where is Caterina, then?" It does not come out as a demand. "Caterina Didac?" I don't mean to be pleading with him.

"My wife?" He looks genuinely perplexed but he did not alter his position. "She is now at home with our daughters."

I tighten up on my grip.

"Ages six and ten," he adds. "They have no livelihood without me."

Cold rain leaks over the collar of my oilskin and runs down my spine. I am shivering like a banshee. I clench my teeth to stop them from chattering.

"Your wallet," I shout. "Give me your wallet!"

Without moving his hand he lets go of the flowers and they flush away in the torrent. Moving slowly like a metronome, he reaches into his coat and retrieves a billfold the size of a small book. I snatch it from him and step back to rifle the contents.

"I can get more money for you if you wish." He speaks in a calm, matter-of-fact tone.

I tear through his identification papers and credit cards and flip through the plastic slots where men keep family photos. I find her there—a studio-quality portrait that is now getting ruined in the rain.

I hold the picture to his face. "Did you kill her?"

"My wife? Why on Gods earth would a man ever kill his wife?"

"You! You are Arnau Didac, who killed your wife because she was unfaithful to you!"

He dropped his umbrella to his side and stood as resolute as a bowman on the storm prow, leaning into the full force of the weather.

I raise my pistol to halt his advance. My thumb is nearly numb but I manage to pull the hammer back, it's distinctive metallic click rings through the gales unrelenting howl.

"My wife, sir, is Catalán. Never would she violate the sacred vows of our marriage. Never! Rob me if you must. Shoot me if you will. Before you do, you will retract the insult you have made to my wife!"

The cloak of rain draws more thickly around us. Water is blurring my vision.

"Turn around!" I bark.

He holds fast and speaks slowly. "You are going to have to shoot me in the face, sir. If you choose to do so, do it like a man."

A headstone at my heel takes my balance. Unknowingly I am stepping backwards, his face still at the business end of my gun barrel. He stands as solid as a statue among the rain-washed graves of his ancestors while all that I can hear pounding at me in the torrent were the words "Fuck! Fuck! Fuck!" in my own voice.

The space between us grows darker as the distance increases. The ferocious, grey Patagonian tantrum is mercilessly pelting, hammering, screaming, blowing me all the way back to the exact same fucked up guy I was on the floor of *The Rooster and The Pig*.

- Marc Hess

How I Spent My Summer

My mom ran the wet cloth over the empty tables, too casually. She had a plan. She called me over to her with just that little tip of the head. "Get him out of here," she whispered. "Take him to the drugstore with you just for now. I need you to pick up my medicine."

I followed her behind the counter, and she stuffed the money into my pocket. She pinned me with those eyes, the same as his, only steadier. The look meant she was handing over her baby brother, my baby uncle, just out of prison. Like she had just tossed me my own personal grenade to carry around for the whole summer vacation.

My uncle resisted getting out of his chair. He complained to the world about his hard life simply with a sigh and his wobbly walk, a druggy habit of movement he had even when he was sober. Our little world would take that walk personally, along with his silence and his eyes that didn't meet anybody else's. It all said he didn't give a damn.

It was a straight shot to the drugstore, about a dozen blocks. Twice we passed guys chilling at a corner, and twice he started conversations which went nowhere and then cut off abruptly, as if to show the boys around here that they lacked all significance for him. Sometimes he'd just lean against a wall and look bored, and I'd have to urge him along. Bystanders would look.

People cut me slack here because a lot of them know me from school. They know I'm LD and ADD and don't care much, but I could see my uncle totaling up a score of attention. Curiosity first, then anger. Their new neighbor now. And my problem.

Whatever happened would have to happen soon. The longer he stayed around, the more it would be my fault when he did screw up. But if he got into trouble soon my mom would probably think I hadn't gotten used to handling him, that I just hadn't enough practice being his chaperone.

We marched along. Or I marched and my uncle tottered, making a show of his fatal lack of respect, talking too loudly when he talked, keeping quiet when he should at least have said something to somebody.

Sometimes he'd get the idea to go into one of the stores on our route, but I kept him moving. This wasn't the Stations of the Cross, I told him. But it felt like he was my Jesus and I had to lug him, cross and all, down all those blocks to the drugstore, his Golgotha, "the place of the skulls," as they say in church. Or I would be lugging him around all summer.

At the drugstore, I gave the man the prescription, and he said it would be about ten minutes. "No problem," I said. It was actually just enough time.

My uncle plopped himself down in the seat by the blood pressure machine, but I said no, come on, let's just look around. He sighed again and pushed his bony body up out of the seat and followed me up and down the aisles, jabbering about this and that. Up and down every single aisle.

When they called our name on the loudspeaker, I cut around behind him and looked in his pockets, and it was just as I had hoped. I walked faster toward the counter, and I gave the man that look, kind of like the one my mom had given me, the one about paying close attention.

We exchanged the money for the medicine, and my baby uncle and I walked toward the door, with the man following us casually, just a little bit behind, so that it was clear when we went out the door that my uncle was out without paying. And clear sailing for me after the police came. I took my solo walk back home that day, with a happy summer stretching out all the way to September.

- Ann Birch

Reverse Engineering

I think that I know what
I needed:
better advice

at an earlier age
ergo the long Ys
branching into the future

and now
the river
winding back
to my youth

I write the poem
so you will know
how beautiful
how green

- Chryss Yost

We Didn't

It didn't happen the day we stayed in Wilmington, walked hand-in-hand on the beach after a seafood dinner at sunset. You kept saying how nice the day had been, almost as if you were surprised by your luck.

You'd booked a hotel for the night. I showered to remove the salt from my body. You stepped into the shower, too.

But we didn't there, not even after we patted each other dry and touched each other on top of sheets. We talked about how we'd have sex if we could, but we went to bed virgins again.

And not the time we sat across from each other on the couch, our legs next to each other. We were in your apartment, Buhl Apartments. An elderly woman lived in an apartment beneath you, so we tried to be quiet so as not to disturb her.

I knew in that moment we'd be together forever. I'd always heard people say you know when you know. That feeling, that knowing, pinned itself. Yes, him, it said.

When we kissed, it was different somehow. I wanted to crawl inside you. My mouth couldn't drink you enough. Your hands were on me, you'd blinded yourself through our kissing, but your hands knew there were more ways to see.

We could've connected completely, but a voice said no. A voice whispered wrong, wrong, wrong.

Again, again, and again we stopped ourselves when our bodies screamed.

* * *

A few months later, we spent six hours taking wedding photographs before marrying in a church on top of Shiner Hill. The altar had a floor-to-ceiling window. How the treetops burned green, the sun beginning its descent.

Through the reception, I knew that soon there'd be no stopping. I thought about it as I made my way through round tables seated with people we loved, people who'd sat next to us on church benches, wore purity rings stamped True Love Waits and delicate gold crosses around their necks. They all knew, too, didn't they? Did their grins mean they could see behind our closed doors? My dress wasn't pure white, but off with a rum pink border.

We entered our townhouse late that evening, our bed covered in red rose petals scattered by our friends. You helped me take off my ball gown and then showered alone. If you wait, they'd said, your marriage will be blessed.

We'd been to premarital counseling, talked about expectations with our pastor who had us read The Act of Marriage: The Beauty of Sexual Love. We were ready, I thought, but I'd stopped myself for so long I didn't have any yes left in me. I helped guide you in me anyway.

It was over before it really began, before my body loosened. You slept soundly while I stared at the ceiling's starburst point texture. I'd lost two names: my last and virgin. Was this what waiting meant? What more needed to be stripped from me to be allowed to love you?

I went downstairs, ate a bag of Salty Lay's, my belly hungry from all the food it hadn't had that day.

* * *

The truth is, I wish my first time could have been in those freer moments, twenty years now, back with that first whisper in the arms of a man I still love—his hot breath, thick lips, the moment I didn't want to be a virgin anymore.

You could have had me then, the boundary between your body and mine removed, just so I could get closer, be in you as if I were man and you woman, a hunter after prey, chasing through a cave, warm and moist. Not a cringe-worthy moist but for the dampness of your lip, I would've gone anywhere. In a plane, across a bridge, any height for your want. For mine. If only I could have been a fish in the belly of a whale. But no, not like that. Like a piece of green Playdoh pressed to orange, rolled into one new color, brown, because our colors became one. Muddied some might say. I say earthy. Safe.

Dare I say, holy?

But we didn't. Not in Buhl apartments, Wilmington Beach, our apartment before we wed. We didn't because we

120

thought we'd be better somehow—

We died to self, never taught how to be born again in desire, to erase markings labeled wrong. The magic didn't happen when we'd exchanged rings before God, but long before, when spirit first fired.

We believed a lie. I wish I could forget.

- Jamey Temple

THE VENDOR

The man selling watermelons
out the back of his russet pickup

just a lawn dart's toss
from a blurring freeway

lifts up his shirt to show me
the pucker left by a bullet,

says, It's up to me now,
gotta do something worthwhile,

then takes my money
and hands me his best

after wiping it off with
the clean edge of his shirt.

- Michael Meyerhofer

Portrait Of A Zen Monk

While I am trying to finish a poem,
reading back what I have so far,

testing the rhythm and slide of each syllable,
weighing the risk of every reference

to subatomic particles and the maneuvers
of Napoleon's lesser-known marshals,

my cat with equal fervor is trying
to bury his fresh waste in the litter box

just a few yards from my grimace,
patiently committed to his scratching,

utterly defined by what he does
until it's done, then leaves behind.

- Michael Meyerhofer

To Keep the Mind Quiet

In the summer that my mother killed herself, I'd been away for just a year. A sense of obligation convinced me to return, the impetus being some repairs and general maintenance needed at her apartment complex. The landlord was a piece of shit. After barely making it through high school, I'd been offered a job doing some construction work for a friend's father up in Glenn County, in Willows. Over time, I got good at it. The work was tough and didn't leave me time for much else, but it tired my body and kept the mind quiet.

I worried when it got too loud.

The trip from Willows to Modesto was three hours long, but the route itself had only three directions to follow, hardly any turns. That meant a lot of time alone with myself and memories of home, memories for which I rarely made the time. In particular, I thought about the dogs that used to roam around the neighborhood. The place was filled with strays, dogs abandoned or set loose by selfish, careless owners too fucked-up for pets. When I was fourteen, I took a shaggy, pepper-haired stray back home with me. She was the most pathetic-looking of the lot. I fed her a package of lunch meat, turkey, I think, and drew her a bath, playing with her as the water did its work to wash away the fleas and dirt matted on her fur. She was looking pretty good, but when I went to towel her off, she shook, and then her eyes rolled backwards in her head. My mom came home and found me sopping wet and crying in the bathroom with this random dog panting frantically in my lap. She helped me wrap the dog in a towel, then called animal control to take it away. When they arrived, they wrinkled their foreheads in pity and told me that she probably had parvo.

Anyway, that was running through my mind on the drive to Modesto. Haven't bothered much with dogs since. I saw a few as I arrived at my mother's neighborhood and, like avoiding an ex at the supermarket, I took the long way round.

At my mother's apartment I entered without knocking. We were family and I knew I was expected.

124

"Mom?" I spoke into the empty apartment. Everything was yellow: the peeling laminate floor, the walls, the single-pane windows. Yellow is the sign of age, the quiet passage of time.

"Hm?" she answered from her bedroom.

I didn't know her mood at present, so I approached carefully, stopping short outside her bedroom door. "Did you take your meds today?"

"What a way to greet your mother." She paused and waited for me to respond. I stayed quiet. "No, hon. I don't need it. I told you, that shit makes me heavy."

"Well," I said, only mildly concerned. She seemed calm, at least. "How about dinner? You hungry?"

"I don't know, Hunter. I'm waiting for my body to communicate that information with me."

I took a step forward and pushed open the door to the bedroom. My mother stared upward, eyes unmoving as she took in the curves and colors of the tapestry above her bed, yellow, orange, and red. Thick terry cloth fabric hung weighty against the nails hammered haphazardly into the edges of the tapestry, which had been purchased at a roadside in Kentucky during one of her unplanned excursions. She'd called me the day she got it, rambling on about its similarities to some imagined tapestry of her fictional past. I might have continued to interrogate her on her health, but the odor of skunk that permeated her space communicated to me that her lethargy would soon give way to hunger. Mom was a stoner, which was better for her than being sober, and actually one of our very few shared interests.

In the kitchen I pulled out the phonebook, then dialed for take-out. Meds were more appealing when offered with a meal.

A collection of orange pill bottles, both empty and full, covered the countertops. Labels like Loxitane, Seroquel, and Clozaril were printed in bold black print, each expressed more as a statement than a name. My uncle used to say that the woman who laughed to herself was not the sister he grew up with, but I could never imagine her any other way. I only ever knew my mother as the woman who laughed to herself, cried to herself, saw every action taken by others as some injustice committed against herself. She was the aged musician who claimed music executives had stolen her work, the woman checked periodically into the hospital because she wouldn't stop screaming that Kirk Hammett was framed for the murder of Laci Peterson.

Metallica fans were rioting.

* * *

After calling in an order for Chinese, I stepped out into the thick heat of the Central Valley, dry and arid and made all the worse by smoke drifting ominously from perpetual wildfires. My mother's decrepit apartment, paid almost entirely by government assistance, overlooked a patch of yellow grass and faced the local community college I'd refused to attend. Beyond that, thousands of acres of almond orchards stretched out across the valley, pink and full in spring, but nude and barren by summer.

"Those motherfucking almond trees make me rage," my mother used to say. "It just doesn't make sense to be growing almonds here. It takes so much water. It's fucking nuts."

She'd made that joke when I told her my plans to move north, smoke drifting from a cigarette in her left hand as she lounged in a frayed and faded lawn chair. Something between a chuckle and a cough emphasized just how taxing humor could be.

"Hunter, why don't you just stay? You're gonna go all that way and do what, patch up some drywall? Stay here, Hunter. Go to school there, right here, Hunter. You can stay. You don't have to go."

She'd almost convinced me. For some inexplicable reason, even the slightest moments of coherence and sanity could trick me into believing my mother was normal. *It could be different,* I thought. *I can go to college. Sure, she'll need my help sometimes, but we're family. I can help her. This can work.*

It didn't. That same night, lying on dampened sheets soaked through with the sweat of summer heat, I listened as

126

my mother's manic rambling disassembled the fantasy. Her voice carried from her bedroom, dancing wildly throughout the apartment.

"Nosey Hunter, goddamnit goddamn, Hunter. I'll make you sorry, make you damned sorry, Hunter! I was the belle of the ball, yes I was! Oh, yes I was. Long before that bitch, that little bitch. Gonna fuck her up."

I knew what would come next and closed my eyes, lying on top of my sheets, muscles motionless and tense. After several hours of exhausted crying and laughter, my mother grew silent, and I heard the click of my door being opened. I felt her standing in the doorway, a presence staring in the dark.

"She broke it. That little cunt broke it."

I said nothing as my mother walked toward my bed. She sat down next to me and placed her left hand on the inside of my thighs, fingers moving slick and slow against the sweat.

"Be more quiet than the most quiet you have ever been in your entire life."

I didn't move. I didn't speak. I tried to ignore her. To fight would be to acknowledge.

I kept my eyes closed, but felt my mother's hot breath against my lips as she opened her mouth and kissed me. My lips pursed, and I imagined I was somewhere else, fighting the cry that welled in my chest, in hopes that my mother would think me asleep. My mind was loud.

Moments passed. A small cry escaped from deep within her, both devoid of and filled with meaning. A noise with meaning only I could understand. Her hand stopped rising between my thighs, stopped just beneath the point of no return. It seemed like she was waiting. For what, I'm not sure. Eventually, realizing that I wouldn't respond, that I wouldn't wake to engage with her behavior and partake in the performance, she climbed from my bed and stood solemnly in the doorway.

"We're going to break tradition, Hunter. Break the cycle."

After it happened, I had a dream, or it may have been a thought. I didn't remember falling asleep. I just remembered my uncle and me on a hunting trip in September. We were aiming at a buck, and he told me to be more quiet than the most quiet I've ever been in my entire life.

I left the next morning.

* * *

The Chinese was delivered about a half hour after I called. I walked into the apartment and threw the bag of food down upon my mother's crowded card table, blind as my eyes adjusted to the dark. As they did, she came into view, standing in her doorway down the hall, staring at me sadly.

"Dinner, Mom. I ordered Chinese."

She nodded. "Good, hon. I'm hungry as a hostage."

We ate. She took her meds. I did my duty as a son and made repairs to the apartment. At the end of the week I left Modesto, making empty promises to visit as my mother begged me to stay. I made these promises at a distance, literally and figuratively. I turned my back to leave. Before I made it past the door, my mother snuck a hand onto my shoulder and squeezed it tight. It was the first time she'd touched me since that night in my bedroom. I didn't turn back, and she didn't follow me out.

As I drove through the city for what I knew would be the last time for a long time, I made a wrong turn. Lost in a maze of one-way streets and dead-end turns, I didn't notice the pack of dogs about to run in front of my car until the last second. I slammed on my brakes, cursing as they weaved in and out of traffic, and then I grew quiet at the sight of a shaggy, pepper-haired stray. She was smaller than the one I'd known, a pup. I sat, idling in my car, and watched as she ran with her friends until they'd gone completely out of sight. I found my route pretty quickly after that, but thought again about dogs as I made my way to Willows.

* * *

Three weeks later, I got the call that my mother had died. My uncle found her dead in the tub, a glass coated in antifreeze set carefully on the tiled floor I'd sealed just weeks before with

128

grout.

I don't remember crying, though I'm sure I must have. My uncle offered to make arrangements for a funeral and send me my mother's things, but I didn't like the idea of him invading her space. I remembered my dream, my uncle's hands gripped tight along the rifle, the stock against his shoulder, eyes trained squarely on a buck. I remembered him whispering to me. Over the phone, I lied and told him I'd pack her things on my own. Later, I left a message for her landlord asking him to trash or donate her belongings.

I didn't return to Modesto for a while, but when I did, it was the springtime and almond blossom petals blew in the wind, catching the sunlight in shades of pink and white. I was on my way to a job in the country, in the orchards, and it was the first time I felt I could breathe deeply in the valley. I took it all in and imagined the trees never changed, and everything would stay that new. The thought was loud. It was like music, and I let it sing.

- Jacob Anthony Moniz

It did start early, my head bound in aches

I am only alive to how bad I feel,
like I am the iron skillet banged on
the stovetop, partly because of how heavy it is,
partly to wake the sound of breakfast.
My grief cozies next to me, planted like a garden.
Sometimes I feel so thin
I'm happy to have a roll of fat at my hips,
tethered to the delight of
this planet's ceaseless hunger.

- Samn Stockwell

THE SUICIDE AS A PAINTING
BY JAN STEEN

At the back of his head, villagers are wheeling
their barrows through the lattice of the brain,
hay for sheep traveling through the constricted
arteries near the heart, the arch of the hip,
somewhat chipped, is the resting spot for
a lunching bricklayer. In the dust of the left knee,
a wedding party dancing and drunk,
pulling on the ligaments.

- Samn Stockwell

Old Plains Houses

Unplanned lean-to wooded walls
Full of scattered wind resistance
At edges of ancient wheat fields
Shading empty eaves above dust
Where wind stacks tumbleweeds
At night stars shine through
Beside a highway passing by the way
Drifting sunlight over fallow fields
Dry roots and weeds surrounding
Hold weakly where they grow
No paint remains on grey wood
Rusty nails barely hold
Barbed wire on door knobs
Won't do to stop intruders
Where few would want to enter
As another spring storm
And a tornado may dip
Down and take the last
Of what was once
Or maybe some developer
Will buy the dilapidated town
And send bulldozers
With much more power
Than years of decay
To provide quick destruction
But there are things you say
Words remembered
By those who lived inside you
Dreamers who moved on
Drifters like all of us

- John Gorman

The Least of My Sins

Another little brown box of an apartment in Kansas. Another roommate who has more going in his life than I. Brice—thin and blue-eyed and alive, hair like fire, a laugh like stars. He did coke just like I did, back before we moved in together. The two of us would blow rails and play *Diablo 2* or *Tekken Tag Tournament* until dawn.

Then he just stopped.

He got a job.

He kept it.

Not in a thousand years could I do this.

Brice wakes each day in the purple dark that whispers of sunrise, puts on a suit and tie, goes to work in Kansas City, comes home around the time I crawl from my cave, dopesick and fiending, to roam the humid nights, meeting one-armed dopefiends under flickering street lamps covered in flies, testing car doors to see if they'll open and give me something to steal. He has money, a vehicle, a girlfriend, a future.

He lives a life I live in my dreams.

* * *

We sit at dinner in the living room, cicadas shrieking in the warm dark outside the balcony, the room's single dim bulb making the yellowing paint on the walls seem to writhe. We are eating Hamburger Helper off an ancient card table of thin brown pleather that creaks with each bite.

With a mouthful of noodles, he speaks. "You know," he says, chewing and swallowing hard. "If you applied those same skills you use to sell drugs, you could get a really good job."

I smile down into my noodles. My throat and tongue are numb. "There's no skill in sellin' coke, man," I say. "The shit sells itself," I say. "You should know that better than anybody."

"I guess," he says.

We eat in silence. I see it then—the gap that separates me from the world. Almost everyone I will ever meet in my life will be like Brice, will be able to take it or leave it alone, will know the secrets to living a life that trends upward, will find relationships and jobs and education and accomplishments attainable with a bit of work and a dose of discipline.

Not me.

"How long you going to be gone for again?" he asks, stabbing up more pasta.

"Two weeks," I say, toying with my food. The cocaine makes my stomach sour. "You'll take care of the guinea pigs, right?" I ask.

My mother had foisted them on me months before as my family moved from Chicago to Dallas for her new job. I was in between. I was supposed to only have them for a few weeks, but they live here now.

The apartment is so small that we can only fit them in the closet behind the kitchen where they live in a huge cage. I turn the closet light on during the day and off at night.

"I thought you hated the things," Brice says. His thick lips smack and slurp.

"I do," I say, staring at his lips. I set my fork down and push my plate away. "They're loud, they're needy, they stink, and they do nothing but cost money," I say, shivering at the thought of having to touch the filthy creatures.

They depend on me in a way total and complete.

I hate them.

I thank all the rough gods of the world that I never had children.

"I'll take care of them," Brice says, looking me in the eyes, smiling.

He's a normal person, right?

I swear that he's normal.

I swear that he's not like me.

It makes his brutality all the worse.

The most vicious men I've ever met were not dope-fiends, but normal people.

Humanity is a cancer.

* * *

I cannot remember where I went on vacation. I cannot remember the names of the girls I've slept with, cannot remember their faces.

But I remember the guinea pigs.

I remember my hatred for being put in such a position, as though my mother was not paying my rent, paying my tuition, buying my food. As though I was not a broke drug dealer who could not turn a profit. As though I wasn't a junky loser who only needed to do this one small thing for his mother, a woman who never gave up on him.

As though she were the burden.

And not me.

I remember that I could never harm them. I remember that I fed them, cleaned their cages. I remember that despite my hatred, I would not let an innocent animal suffer.

What does Brice remember?

* * *

I come home from the trip exhausted, throw my bags onto the stained gray carpet of my room. Brice is walking around the apartment on his cellphone, still wearing his work clothes—baby blue button down shirt, gray tie, dark slacks, shiny black shoes.

I open the closet. One guinea pig is shrieking and shrieking. Their stench is worse than ever. My eyes begin to water.

They are skin and bones.

One does not move.

He has starved them.

"Brice, what the fuck, man!" I scream over my shoulder. He looks at me and shrugs while still on the phone, rolls his eyes. I do not get physical with him.

Or maybe I do.

I cannot remember.

No, I would not get physical.

I am a coward.

I walk up to him. Something in my face makes him

rush the call and hang up.

"You said you didn't want them anymore!" Brice says, looking hurt. "You said you didn't want the damn things!"

"I don't!" I scream, tearing at my hair when I want to tear his throat. "That doesn't mean I want them tortured! You should have just killed them!"

"I thought you'd be happy! At least one is dead, man!" he says.

"Not like this," I say, shaking my head.

* * *

I bury the skinny, shriveled guinea pig in a shallow grave, a little hole in the grass behind our apartment, the residents of the old folks home across the street shuffling out to watch me dig with a hammer, the only tool I could find.

I don't even have a shoebox to bury it in.

It is so light in my hands as I lower it into the dirt.

Such a small thing.

It did not deserve this.

* * *

I feed the other one, get it healthy again, but in time, my disease worsens, and I can no longer afford to keep it.

I do the only thing I can think of.

There is a park where I play disc golf and smoke weed, its rolling hills sloping to a wooded strip that protects the park from the roar of I-70. It is summer, or maybe winter. I remember thinking that it will survive well in this little wood, that it will be okay.

Surely it was not okay.

This is the least of my sins: trusting the welfare of these animals to this ruinous man, then releasing the survivor to certain death.

I doubt Brice remembers any of this.

Why do I?

- Adam Fout

136

CRANES WALKING

I knew nothing
of Franco when I walked
through Spain

in my very short skirt.
Sunburned arms, long
stride. The heat.

Friends sped ahead,
unrecognizable, faces
like slammed-shut

drawers. That's me
in a paisley nightgown,
smoking a last cigarette.

I walked through
a dictator's guarded
streets. Was it two

hundred thousand
people killed?
Now I leave Florida,

final white pelicans
heavy in air, last
roseate spoonbill.

Elegant sandhill cranes
step in front
of my car as if

I'm already gone.
Their cream-colored faces,
their bloodied crowns.

- Barbara Daniels

SLOWLY YOU REMEMBER

Slowly, as an apple
       ripens
Slowly, as a crescent
       rounds

Slowly, as a sky
       darkens
Slowly, as a petal
       browns

Slowly, as a stain
       deepens,
Slowly, as a pond
       scums

Slowly, as a spine
       stiffens
Slowly, as Taps
       sounds

Slowly, as addiction
       thickens
Slowly, as a last breath
       comes

Slowly, slowly you
       awaken
Slowly, the body is
       re-found

Slowly memory turns
       to thought, thinking
follows its sluggish course,
dissolving, slowly, into feeling.

How swift then is the shrinking
       back from knowing.
How swift then regret, remorse.

- Jeanne Julian

SUNSETS

Tom Sekiba lifted up the collar of his polo shirt, hoping for a breeze to dry off the sweat. Daylight lingered well past 8:30 on these June evenings in upstate New York. With the phone pressed to his left ear, the *briiing, briiing* was like a summons—echoing his own mental command. Maybe the old man was in the shower; Saturdays were usually for dancing at the Renton Community Center back in the Pacific Northwest.

Tom watched the sunset through the open kitchen window. The bright red disc was a glare he couldn't blink away, still burning even with his eyelids closed. Almost etched onto his retina, he could see his father—still a handsome man with a full head of hair streaked with black at eighty-five years. Dad had been partnering the three widowed Chin sisters in a never changing foxtrot. Tom could almost hear Glen Miller's saxophone amped up loud for the hard of hearing.

"I take care of myself," Dad had told him how many years back on a visit when the girls were just entering their teens. And the old geezer had. True, Dad hadn't returned to steelhead fishing or golfing but there was Pickle Ball on Mondays and Wednesdays where he'd "cut" the ball into the opponent's court: making his friends run, making them laugh with an out of breath "Oh you!" Once a week, Walt and Aki took turns making reservations for the van to take them to the Little Eagle Casino. If you played the slots for two hours, you got a free buffet lunch with fried chicken wings or piles of easy-to-peel shrimp.

Maureen was rinsing strawberries in a colander. The red and gold of the sunset added a kind of aura to his wife's sleeveless summer dress. Tom watched as she shook the fruit dry. With a paring knife, she began removing the stems and cutting away the spoiled parts. Strawberries and cream. Tom smiled to himself. He was getting close to retirement. One daughter was teaching English in Japan while the other had landed her first real job as a physical therapist.

These, too, should be the best days of his father's life, Tom thought. Dad had survived, but not like his old pals. Rocky Yoshinaka hardly left his room at the Keiro Nursing home, his bad hip limiting him to three steps at a time in a walker. Worse yet was Bill Namba who couldn't even remember his wife's name—just that she was "the Boss."

"Nyah," Dad had complained about the funerals he had attended: Blaine Memorial, St. Peter's, or the Buddhist Temple. He still sent sympathy cards with his koden, a ten dollar bill to help with burial expenses the way Mom had shown him when she was alive. Now her ashes rested in a special bronze urn sitting on the fireplace mantel.

That wasn't what Tom wanted for himself or Maureen. They'd agreed on "Do Not Resuscitate" orders in their Living Wills. When the time came, all he wanted was Maureen holding his hand—just that. But Tom remembered the few times at his dad's house when he'd asked: "Have you thought about any special funeral arrangements?"

His father had glared, pursing his lips together in a tight seam. "You figure out."

Tom's face had flushed hot, the way it always had when he messed up—dropping a fly ball in the baseball tryouts or announcing that he had changed his college major from civil engineering to graphic design. He couldn't ask questions because Dad expected him to know the answers. Dad was so black and white; it was hard to explain subjects like art or volunteering for charity organizations. "Who pay you for all kind squiggly lines?" his father would ask. "Why do that?"

When Mom had been alive, she'd monitored his father's blood pressure. How she'd nagged at him about too much salt, too much sugar. But as Dad had pointed out so many times later, nothing she did could have stopped her breast cancer. Dad was always clicking his tongue: "Worry, worry, worry. That what kill her."

A flock of crows landed in the crown of the old willow tree. They cawed to each other, taking mincing steps down towards the trunk. Tom was up to seven rings on the phone. He considered excuses for why the old man wasn't answering: showering, napping? Maybe the Chin sisters had invited him to play Mexican Trains. When Tom called on Saturdays, he'd tried to show an interest in his father's routine. It was the same every week: breakfasts at the 321 Café, the price of Ramen noodles at Maruta, the funny joke Aki told. Sometimes Tom wondered why he called at all. What bothered him was the tone of the old man's voice. Tom felt he was always being talked at, barely uttering an "uh huh" or "yeah" that meant his father should continue. All their phone calls were one-way streets.
140

One of the crows leaned forward into a series of squawks. Maureen glanced out the window, towards the sound. Who was he kidding? Phone calls to his father were always a downer, but it was something that had to be done.

A longtime grandfather now, the old man did ask questions about the girls. Half-white, because of Maureen, Dad figured Sandra and Amy would marry out. "Why," his father asked, "no date more Japanese boys? Their kids going to be only one-quarter. That tiny bit! What left?" But the way he spoke, Tom noticed, was sad now. Not angry. Like he was slowly giving in to the inevitable.

These last few weeks, Dad was sounding more tired. Tom's oldest sister had been making arrangements for a surprise visit at Thanksgiving—all the brothers and sisters together with their kids. Tom rubbed his forehead; it would be a nightmare cramming into Dad's unkempt rambler. The last time Tom had visited, his sister Gail had been there, too, cleaning out Mom's clutter. He couldn't help but notice how his father seemed to shrink into his favorite armchair—more alone amidst his children.

Maureen's porcelain bowl was a quarter full of sliced fruit, bright red staining her fingertips. Tom reached over to snag a strawberry, popping it into his mouth. "Stop that," she smiled. Then noticing his slow chewing, she asked: "No answer? Maybe you dialed wrong."

That's when the other end picked up. Tom put one hand on the kitchen counter to steady himself.

A soft voice, barely audible, mumbled: "'Lo."

It was hard to make out the word, to recognize his father—the feisty soldier who had lugged a machine gun through World War II, the blunt disciplinarian who always seemed to be yelling. Tom ran his hand through his hair.

All he could say was, "Dad?"

His face burned with the old shame from having moved so far away. But each of his siblings had—to San Diego, Denver, even Hawaii. Tom remembered how his father had nodded his head when Tom told him he was moving to New York: "You have your own lives now." It still surprised Tom to hear how many Japanese and Chinese women insisted on cooking for Dad when the old man smacked his lips, mentioning how he missed Hom Bau or somen with just the right taste—aji. "They don't have husbands to cook for anymore,"

Dad would explain.

"Don't come. I be all right," his father plunged into the conversation.

Why, Tom wondered, did he always feel like he was missing the subject—talked over or talked down to. Communication over the phone was always a minefield, ready to go off at any minute. No respect, that's what his father hated the most. And it was getting harder, what with his father's growing deafness. Tom had told Maureen once: "It's like he only hears these bits and pieces. In his head, they don't add up to how I mean them."

Gently, Tom tried to prod some details with the old standby question: "What have you been doing? Wasn't today dancing?"

There was an exasperated sigh on the other end like a balloon leaking air. "Nothing! I do nothing. Why you think it take me so long to get to the phone? I feel lousy." The words exploded in Tom's ear. "Today, Aki's boy was going to take us out for big sushi dinner, too. I really wanted to go. But have to say no."

Maureen was watching his face. As she shook her head, her long brown hair slid over a shoulder. She pointed with one red finger to her head, her eyebrows raised up in a question. The index finger moved down to her chest, then to her stomach.

"Is it a headache," he started to ask. "This is Tom, you know."

The voice on the other end became shrill, whiny: "I not crazy yet. I no forget you call on Saturdays. Why you always want to put me away?"

"Dad, I didn't say anything like that." Tom pulled up a bar stool and eased himself upon the seat cushion, heels on the footrest. Maureen dried her hands on a kitchen towel. Then she walked over to knead Tom's shoulders. He took a deep breath. Maureen was right; he needed to start over. "I'm sorry you're not feeling well. I won't interrupt. Just talk to me."

There was a suspicious pause. "You don't know nothing," his father continued.

Tom pictured the way an old man's lips dribbled spittle. Dad was probably in his pajamas, missing his dentures, one side of his hair flattened down. Breath rattled on the other end. There was the sound of coughing, hawking up phlegm,

142

and spitting.

Maureen tilted her head to catch the sounds from the telephone. She murmured: "That doesn't sound good." Tom patted her hand. Her fingers felt cold from the rinse water. Tom told himself, he could be good at waiting. He nodded at his wife, but he didn't speak.

"Damn bloody stuff. In bed, I hot—cold—hot—cold. Start when? Week ago? Say to self, maybe Vienna sausage bad. Maybe it all mix up in stomach with scrambled eggs I try to use up. Sit on benjo long time. Oshide hurt. Diarrhea."

As his father spoke, Tom remembered the smells of the hospital when he sat beside Mom's bed. Blood and urine were the dirty business of living. Monitoring wires and tubes had run across her chest and arms. *She's so thin*, the doctor had said. *There's only one sweet spot on her left arm for an intravenous line. We're saving that.* Each day seemed like a lifetime with the effort to smile against the bad news.

Tom sat listening, trying to see his father's point-of-view, not offering any suggestions—just nodding his head. The old man's voice lost its momentum, wandering in his complaints. Most of all, Dad said that he felt tired—winded: "Not hurt too bad. Just no go juice." Then beginning again, slowly, as if for the first time: "You the brave one. Before the end, you tell me—why hurt so much? It time to let me go. Please, you say. That word, 'please'. All these year later, I think you hurt long time because of me."

Tom heard the loneliness in his father's voice. He swallowed against the tightness in his throat, against the strawberry seeds still between his teeth, wanting to say, "It's not your fault." But Maureen put one finger across his lips. She shook her head, mouthing the words *not yet*. That's when Tom realized his father was talking to his mother.

Outside, the sun had set but the backlight against the hills gave off a glow. A light breeze blew the day-warmed air through the kitchen. The crows had become almost invisible against the shadows of the willow's canopy, but Tom knew they were still there. He could hear their random chatter.

"When you watch TV, how come you switch station without asking me?" The questions were becoming more random. The voice on the phone seemed more than a light year away, growing fainter.

Tom covered the telephone's mouthpiece with his

palm. When Maureen spoke, it was to say "9-1-1?" But who would open the door for the paramedics? They'd put oxygen under his nose, lifting Dad onto a gurney and speeding him to the hospital. An old man next to Mom's bed had cried: "Someone, anyone. I have to pee." Tom lowered his head, chin resting almost against his chest.

Alzheimer's. Dementia. Simple old age. How long, Tom thought, can one keep both mind and body going? Even though he could feel Maureen's warmth as she stood so close to him on this fine summer evening, Tom felt empty and helpless. He wasn't sure he had anything to give. The doctors hadn't helped his mother with their morphine that took the pain away only for a few hours. She'd had to wait, curled into a tight ball, before the next injection. Ever since he was a boy, Tom had heard the phrase from Dad and all of Dad's friends: a good death. That was Fleazy Noji who had a heart attack as he watered his garden. Fleazy had been found face up, unseeing eyes staring into the blue sky. That was Sophie Oishi's aneurysm, her hands flailing up as she sunk to the ground while she played with her grandson in the park.

Tom put the phone back up to his ear. He cleared his voice, imagining Dad looking out the living room window. Tom wondered where the sun was in the Northwest sky. He made himself sound agreeable, keeping his words clear and short. "You're a tough guy, Dad." Tom could see the pinched V of Maureen's eyebrows as he said: "No hospital for you, right?"

"Yeah," his father wheezed. Then began another bout of coughing.

Maureen asked in her quiet way: "Are you sure, Tom?"

There was nothing the doctors could do to fix worn-out parts. A good death would let you go quickly. It was natural, Tom thought, just you and time. He nodded to Maureen. There was so much he wanted to say in this one lucid moment, but didn't. "Dad," he said into the phone's mouthpiece, "You're tired. Why don't you lie down? Take a good long nap."

Maybe it was the short sentences he used. Maybe his father finally heard a suggestion he agreed with. Maybe it was his tone of voice. Dad answered: "You know, Tommy, I think I do that."

The whole house was dark except for the thin light of the stars reflecting off the refrigerator. Maureen put her arms around his waist, head resting on Tom's shoulder. It was a car-ing gesture, but it didn't help. Tom could still hear that final click when his father hung up. Tom kept leaning on the counter, listening to the dial tone.

- Sharon Hashimoto

CATCHING YOUR ATTENTION

If words became those thin necked bowling pin things
the circus clowns juggle five at a time
and then in pairs from distanced center ring spots
and for the finale, a quartet flipping
three each across the ring to one another
and the leader flipped in three long handled
blades reflecting flashes from overhead lights

If words were like that and I had ever
learned to juggle or just once run away
to join the circus, perhaps my poem
would twirl and flash and catch the light and your
closer attention before you flipped forward
to the featured full color photographs
of surrealist street graffiti

- Milton Jordan

Cancún

I, too, have felt the deep, unyielding cold,
craved the refuge of a bowl-shaped moon,
its sweet liquor sloshing out, and warm
wet sand. Once I gazed at a tiny snow globe,
emptied myself of everything but want, slipped
the treasure in my coat. My child-heart clanged
like a furnace, shame its terrible heat.
So many things I've ruined: friendships, jobs,
a couple of trips I wish I could take back.
1993, Cancún. I don't recall
too much, though I still cringe. The word washed up
again on my morning walk, so I knelt
and pressed it to my ear. But the sound it made
was the same, hollow and sad as a bassoon.

- Jackleen Holton

WORD TO REMEMBER WHEN THE MOON IS FULL

It looks almost translucent, the early moon,
as if it were made of dark crystal, an ornament

suspended between branches. This evening
I feel like that, see-through, breakable.

All day we moved in wide circles
around each other. Last night, before

the gravitational pull drew us down
into the old argument, a dragonfly

danced with me under the canopy of a tree
draped in lights. I expected the night

to stay magical. Now we have a safe word,
not for sex, like the more-adventurous

couples, but for words themselves,
the way we ball them up and hurl

them, their pitches and tones. We hope
it will save us, these four silly syllables

to bring us back to ourselves before
there's too much to take back.

Because there will be another night like last,
the vino too full of veritas, a dragonfly dancing

into a spider's loom, clouds like gnarled hands
moving over the crystal face of the moon.

- Jackleen Holton

OLD GIRLFRIENDS

I'm driving around with three old girlfriends, a blonde, a brunette and a redhead. I make them laugh. That's why they were my girlfriends, because they thought I was funny. We each married other people, and some of us are on our second marriages.

The car, a twenty-year-old Thunderbird, overheats easily. The city sun heats the black interior, sticking skin to seats. We drive until we hit cornfields and small rustic farm towns. We park a long way from a sprawling neo-classic theater, people converging from all sides.

Inside, it's dark and cool. The movie's not funny, but I am. I sit among the girls saying and doing things that make them giggle. Anything out of the ordinary sets them off. It works best if caught up in the tragedy on the screen.

When the movie ends, we move into the lobby where people mill. As I leave to retrieve the car, the girls are full of lipstick smiles and forgotten beauty.

The sun beats down hotter and brighter than ever. I walk to where I remember parking the car, but it's not there. I find other Thunderbirds sporting different taillights and various colors. I walk for another half hour, but cannot find the car.

I return to the girls. In the theater's spacious foyer, I float through crowds entering or exiting. Hundreds of people slide back and forth in and out of theaters.

"Thomas! Thomas!" I hear, then see, my three old girlfriends running towards me.

"I can't find the car."

"It doesn't matter," says one.

"Should we see another movie?" asks another.

"You go in," I say, "while I check the commercial parking lots. I'll pick you up later or meet you inside."

They join the throng, and I lose them to dark interior. Outside and around a corner, I climb a narrow horizontal concrete staircase to the first floor of a sweaty garage. Acres of metallic colors spread out before me. I weave through yellows, blues and oranges muted by cement walls, ceiling and floor. A long way off I can barely see the outside light trying to penetrate.

I climb another flight of stairs. Up here, yellow looks nearly indistinguishable from red. Daylight appears faint and far away, so I may be imagining it.

Up another flight. No light here except a luminous glow radiating from boxes that might be cars. I go over to one and look in. Bones, perhaps human.

I descend the narrow stairway, swing back to the theater, and sweep through the lobby and into one screening room after another until I find the girls. In the blackness punctuated with film light, people look the same. One room watches a comedy. Everyone's laughing. People are jammed in the back of the auditorium and sit in the aisles. I spot my old girlfriends up front and push through the room, trying to get to them.

Finally I give up and retreat, leaving the laughter for the lobby and bright outdoors. I'll find the car and come back for them. I then spend hours going up and down broad ivory avenues that in the heyday of farming and small town factories hummed with life. Today, not so much. Still, approximate hues and models deceive me. I imagine the area where I parked my car. My mind sees it, but I must have been too busy impressing the girls to take note of the location.

I give up and return to the theater that by now has lost its Greek look. Instead, a post-modern squarish box squats in its place, all oblique angles and shallow steps. Moviegoers chat quietly. The sun's intensity has, if anything, increased. I weave through cliques looking for my party of three, but everyone's a stranger.

I give up and back out. The avenues, fewer and wider than ever, are interrupted by expansive fields sprouting corn, wheat and soy. Crossing earthen land to farther and farther avenues that surely lead to other fields and avenues beyond, I languish in the light blue sky above and the green and yellow plants below.

- Richard Holinger

Sappho Edges Toward the Cliff

Sappho looked over the cliff ledge to blue-green waters churning below. With one more step she would be embroiled in waves, the thrashing, breaking, slamming rampage second only to the harsh, disjointed crush of love, that furious roar of exultation Phaon fed her in field, pool, and bed, her body unleashed from mind, limbs gone spastic, mouth, tongue, fingers, toes, eyes, hair, knuckles, knees fusing with his, lying, kneeling, sitting.

She balked. Yes, the boy had spurned her, his ancient lover who'd taught him pleasure with the discipline and ease of the naming of plants. But was the ingrate worth the fall to salt-water pools, his selfish lusting for other bodies more supple in the acrobatics of love, a face not masked with wrinkles, a heart unfettered by caution, suspicion, and rage?

Sappho stepped back. Her students would understand. Those under her tutelage, those who greeted her mornings in desperate longing to belong, those who proffered wonder at her womanhood, those who sang along with her in heavenly voices to the lyre strummed to the meter's beat. If old age dyed hair silver, locked knees helpless, provoked her nights and oppressed her days, it would also save her, hug her backward, away from the rending of body and soul. Her solace would come from words of grief, of loss, of loneliness, from their longing to find their way into song, the lyrics leaping, hurling themselves from her throat, more glorious airborne than any remaining mired on silenced land.

That, and the warm skin's touch of a young woman's breasts on hers.

- Richard Holinger

Contributors

Montana Agte-Studier   New York NY

D. Michael Armstrong   San Antonio TX

Ann Birch   El Paso TX

Laurie Blauner   Seattle WA

John Bradley   DeKalb IL

Gordon Brown   Las Vegas NV

Mary Byrne   Montpellier, Occitanie France

Ann Casapini   Tuckahoe NY

Renu Chopra   Tarzana CA

Stanley Crawford   Albuquerque NM

Barbara Daniels   Sicklerville NJ

Alfred Fournier   Phoenix AZ

Adam Fout   Southlake TX

John Garmon   Las Vegas NV

Geoffrey Graves   Laguna Beach CA

Sharon Hashimoto   Tukwila WA

Marc Hess   Fredericksburg TX

Richard Holinger   Saint Chalres IL

Jackleen Holton   San Diego CA

Milton Jordan   Georgetown TX

Jeanne Julian   South Portland ME

Karen McPherson   Eugene OR

Michael Meyerhofer   Fresno CA

Jacob Anthony Moniz   Roseland IN

Giorgia Pavlidou   Claremont CA

Huddlestone Phillips   Amsterdam Holland

Oscar Rodriguez   Austin TX

Federica Santini   Atlanta GA

Dan Smart   Chicago IL

Austin Smith   Schapville IL

Matthew J. Spireng   Kington NY

Samn Stockwell   Barre VT

Tessa Swackhammer   Hamilton, Ontario Canada

Jamey Temple   Williamsburg KY

Charmaine Arjoonlal   Whitehorse Yukon Canada

Chryss Yost   Santa Barbara CA

SUBMISSIONS FOR THE INAGURAL
JOSHUA TREE NOVEL PRIZE
SUBMISSIONS OPEN: JANUARY 1,2023
SUBMISSIONS CLOSE: APRIL 20,2023

WINNER RECEIVES $2000 AND PUBLICATION
Plus - 20 copies & 20 press packs to reviewers

Guidelines:

> The entry fee is $70.
> All entrants will receive a copy of the winning novel.
> All finalists will be considered for publication.
> Submit the first 10,000 words of your completed man-uscript plus a synopsis of no more than 2500 words
> Do not put your name or any identifying markings, in the body or title of the submission.
> All submissions received through Submittable.
> We adhere to the ethical standards suggested by the Community of Literary Magazines and Publishers (CLMP). Finalists will be selected using a double-concealed reading.
> The editorial staff of Kallisto Gaia Press will select five finalists to forward to the guest judge.

> More info available at:

www.kallistogaiapress.org